PUFFIN BOOKS

MOOMINLAND MIDWINTER

In the winter Moomins always sleep from November to April when the warm weather starts again. But one year something extra-ordinary happens to Moomintroll: he wakes up and finds he can't go to sleep again. He tries rousing Moomin-mamma but she doesn't wake up even when he pulls her ear and shouts at her. Poor Moomintroll is terribly lonely. There's nothing to eat and no one to talk to at home so he goes out – straight into the first snowdrift he had ever seen.

This hauntingly imaginative story of Moomintroll's first winter awake is a perennial favourite.

Tove Jansson studied oil painting in Finland, Sweden and France. She drew the very first Moomin to tease her little brother by drawing the ugliest creature she could – later the Moomin developed a nicer snout and character! She and her mother and brother are the only inhabitants of a little island in the Gulf of Finland, an hour's rowing from the next island.

MOOMINLAND MIDWINTER

WRITTEN AND ILLUSTRATED BY
TOVE JANSSON

Translated by Thomas Warburton

PUFFIN BOOKS

PUFFIN BOOKS

Published by the Penguin Group
Penguin Books Ltd, 27 Wrights Lane, London W8 5TZ, England
Penguin Books USA Inc., 375 Hudson Street, New York, New York 10014, USA
Penguin Books Australia Ltd, Ringwood, Victoria, Australia
Penguin Books Canada Ltd, 10 Alcorn Avenue, Toronto, Ontario, Canada M4V 3B2
Penguin Books (NZ) Ltd, 182–190 Wairau Road, Auckland 10, New Zealand

Penguin Books Ltd, Registered Offices: Harmondsworth, Middlesex, England

First published by Ernest Benn Ltd, 1958
Published in Puffin Books 1971
15 17 19 20 18 16

Printed in England by Clays Ltd, St Ives plc
Set in Linotype Plantin

TO MY MOTHER

INCIDENTS

Moomin Valley in Winter

CHAPTER 1

The snowed-up drawing-room

THE sky was almost black, but the snow shone a bright blue in the moonlight.

The sea lay asleep under the ice, and deep down among the roots of the earth all small beasts were sleeping and dreaming of spring. But spring was quite a bit away because the year had only just got a little past New Year.

At the point where the valley began its soft slope towards the mountains, stood a snowed-up house. It looked very lonely and rather like a crazy drift of snow. Quite near it ran a bend of the river, coal-black between ice-edges. The current kept the stream open all winter. But there were no tracks leading over the bridge, and no one had touched the snowdrifts around the house.

Inside, the house was warm and cosy. Heaps of peat were quietly smouldering in the central-heating stove

11

down in the cellar. The moon looked in sometimes at the drawing-room window, lighting on the white winter covers of the chairs and on the cut-glass chandelier in its white gauze bag. And in the drawing-room also, grouped around the biggest porcelain stove of the house, the Moomin family lay sleeping their long winter sleep.

They always slept from November to April, because such was the custom of their forefathers, and Moomins stick to tradition. Everybody had a good meal of pine-needles in their stomachs, just as their ancestors used to have, and beside their beds they had hopefully laid out everything likely to be needed in early spring. Spades, burning-glasses and films, wind-gauges and the like.

The silence was deep and expectant.

Every now and then somebody sighed and curled deeper down under the quilt.

The streak of moonlight wandered from rocking-chair to drawing-room table, crawled over the brass knobs of the bed end and shone straight in Moomintroll's face.

And now something happened that had never happened before, not since the first Moomin took to his hibernating den. Moomintroll awoke and found that he couldn't go back to sleep again.

He looked at the moonlight and the ice-ferns on the window. He listened to the humming of the stove in the cellar and felt more and more awake and astonished. Finally he rose and padded over to Moominmamma's bed.

He pulled at her ear very cautiously, but she didn't awake. She just curled into an uninterested ball.

'If not even Mother wakes up it's no use trying the others,' Moomintroll thought and went along by himself

12

on a round through the unfamiliar and mysterious house. All the clocks had stopped ages ago, and a fine coat of dust covered everything. On the drawing-room table still stood the soup-tureen with pine-needles left over from November. And inside its gauze dress the cut-glass chandelier was softly jingling to itself.

All at once Moomintroll felt frightened and stopped short in the warm darkness beside the streak of moon-light. He was so terribly lonely.

'Mother! Wake up!' Moomintroll shouted. 'All the world's got lost!' He went back and pulled at her quilt.

But Moominmamma didn't wake up. For a moment her dreams of summer became uneasy and troubled, but she wasn't able to open her eyes. Moomintroll curled up on her bed-mat, and the long winter night went on.

*

At dawn the snowdrift on the roof began to move. It went slithering down a bit, then it resolutely coasted over the roof edge and sat down with a soft thump.

Now all the windows were buried, and only a weak, grey light found its way inside. The drawing-room looked more unreal than ever, as if it were deep under the earth.

Moomintroll pricked his ears and listened long. Then he lit the night-light and padded along to the chest of drawers to read Snufkin's spring letter. It lay, as usual, under the little meerschaum tram, and it was very much like the other spring letters that Snufkin had left behind when he went off to the South each year in October.

It began with the word 'Cheerio' in his big round hand. The letter itself was short:

13

Sleep well and keep your pecker up. First warm spring day
you'll have me here again. Don't start the dam building
without me.

SNUFKIN.

Moomintroll read the letter several times, and suddenly he felt hungry.

He went out in the kitchen. It too was miles and miles
under the earth as it were and looked dismally tidy and
empty. The larder was just as desolate. He found nothing
there, except a bottle of loganberry syrup that had
fermented, and half a packet of dusty biscuits.

Moomintroll made himself comfortable under the
kitchen table and began to chew. He read Snufkin's letter
once more.

After that he stretched out on his back and looked at
the square wooden clumps under the table corners. The
kitchen was silent.

'Cheerio,' whispered Moomintroll. 'Sleep well and
keep your pecker up. First warm spring day,' he said,
slightly louder. And then he sang at the top of his voice:
'You'll have me here again! You'll have me here, and
spring's in the air, and it's warm and fair, and we'll be
here, and there we are, and here and there in any
year ...'

He stopped short when he caught sight of two small
eyes that gleamed out at him from under the sink.

He stared back, and the kitchen was silent as before.
Then the eyes disappeared.

'Wait,' Moomintroll shouted, anxiously. He crept towards the sink, softly calling all the while:

'Come out, won't you? Don't be afraid! I'm good. Come back . . .'

But whoever it was that lived under the sink didn't come back. Moomintroll laid out a string of biscuit crumbs on the floor and poured out a little puddle of loganberry syrup.

When he came back to the drawing-room the crystals in the ceiling greeted him with a melancholy jingle.

'I'm off,' Moomintroll said sternly to the chandelier. 'I'm tired of you all, and I'm going south to meet Snufkin.' He went to the front door and tried to open it, but it had frozen fast.

He ran whining from window to window and tried them all, but they also stuck hard. And so the lonely Moomintroll rushed up to the attic, managed to lift the chimney-sweep's hatch, and clambered out on to the roof.

A wave of cold air received him.

He lost his breath, slipped and rolled over the edge.

And so Moomintroll was helplessly thrown out in a strange and dangerous world and dropped up to his ears in the first snowdrift of his experience. It felt unpleasantly prickly to his velvet skin, but at the same time his snout caught a new smell. It was a more serious smell than any he had felt before, and slightly frightening. But it made him wide awake and greatly interested.

The valley was enveloped in a kind of grey twilight. It also wasn't green any longer, it was white. Everything that had once moved had become immobile. There were no living sounds. Everything angular was now rounded.

'This is snow,' Moomintroll whispered to himself. 'I've heard about it from Mother, and it's called snow.'

Without Moomintroll knowing a thing about it, at that moment his velvet skin decided to start growing woollier. It decided to become, by and by, a coat of fur for winter use. That would take some time, but at least the decision was made. And that's always a good thing.

Meanwhile Moomintroll was laboriously plodding along through the snow. He went down to the river. It was the same river that used to scuttle, transparent and

jolly, through Moomintroll's summer garden. Now it looked quite unlike itself. It was black and listless. It also belonged to this new world in which he didn't feel at home.

For safety's sake he looked at the bridge. He looked at the mail box. They tallied with memory. He raised the lid a little, but there was no mail, except a withered leaf without a word on it.

He was already becoming used to the winter smell. It didn't make him feel curious any more.

He looked at the jasmine bush that was an untidy tangle of bare sprigs, and he thought: 'It's dead. All the world has died while I slept. This world belongs to somebody else whom I don't know. Perhaps to the Groke. It isn't made for Moomins.'

He hesitated for a moment. Then he decided that he would feel still worse if he were the only one awake among the sleeping.

And that was why Moomintroll made the first tracks in the snow, over the bridge and up the slope. They were very small tracks, but they were resolute and pointed straight in among the trees, southwards.

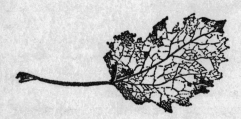

CHAPTER 2

The bewitched bathing-house

Down by the sea, farther to the west, a young squirrel was skipping aimlessly about in the snow. He was quite a foolish little squirrel who liked to think of himself as 'the squirrel with the marvellous tail'.

As a matter of fact, he never thought at all about anything for very long. Mostly he just had a feeling about things. His latest feeling was that his mattress in the nest was getting knobbly, and so he had gone out to look for a new one.

Now and again he mumbled: 'A mattress,' to keep himself from forgetting what he was looking for. He forgot things very easily.

The squirrel went skipping this way and that, in among trees and out on the ice, he stuck his nose in the snow and pondered, looked up at the sky and shook his head and skipped along again.

He came to the cave on the hill and skipped inside. But when he had got there he wasn't able to concentrate any longer, and so he forgot all about his mattress. Instead he sat down on his tail and began to think that people could just as well call him 'the squirrel with the marvellous whiskers'.

Behind the great snowdrift at the opening of the cave somebody had spread out straw on the floor. And in the straw stood a large cardboard box with the lid partly raised.

'That's strange,' said the squirrel aloud, with some surprise. 'That cardboard box wasn't here before. Must be something wrong about it. Or else this is the wrong cave. Or I might be the wrong squirrel, but I wouldn't like to believe that.'

He poked up a corner of the lid and put his head inside the box.

It was warm, and it seemed to be filled with something soft and nice. Suddenly the squirrel remembered his mattress. His small, sharp teeth cut into the soft stuffing and pulled out a flock of wool.

He pulled out one flock after the other; he soon had his arms full of wool and was working hard with all four paws. He felt extremely pleased and happy.

Then all at once someone was trying to bite the squirrel in the leg. Like a streak of lightning he whizzed out of the box, then hesitated for a moment and decided to feel more curious than scared.

Presently an angry head with tousled hair appeared in the hole he had bitten in the wool.

'Are you all there, *you*! ? !' said Little My.

'I'm not sure,' said the squirrel.

'Now you've waked me,' Little My continued severely. 'And eaten half my sleeping-bag. What's the great idea?'

But the squirrel was so beside himself that he had forgotten his mattress again.

Little My gave a snort and climbed out of the cardboard box. She closed the lid on her sister, who was still asleep, and went over and felt the snow with her paw.

'So this is what it's like,' she said. 'Funny ideas people get.' She squeezed a snowball and hit the squirrel on the head with her first throw. And then Little My stepped out from the cave to take possession of the winter.

The first thing she accomplished was to slip on the icy cliff and sit down very hard.

'I see,' Little My said in a threatening voice. '*They* think they'll get away with anything.'

Then she happened to think of what a My looks like with her legs in the air, and she chuckled to herself for quite a while. She inspected the cliff and the hillside and thought a bit. Then she said: 'Well, now,' and did a jumpy switchback slide far out on the smooth ice.

She repeated this six times more and noticed that it made her tummy cold.

Little My went back into the cave and turned her

sleeping sister out of the cardboard box. My had never seen a toboggan, but she had a definite feeling that there were many sensible ways of using a cardboard box.

As to the squirrel, he was sitting in the wood and looking distractedly from one tree to another.

Not for the tail of him could he remember in which one he lived, nor what he had gone out to look for.

*

Moomintroll hadn't come very far south when darkness was already creeping under the trees.

At every step his paws sank deep in the snow, and the snow was not in the least as exciting as it had been.

The silence and the stillness of the wood were complete. Only now and then a large sheaf of snow came thumping down from a tree. The branch from which it had fallen rocked a while, and then all was lifeless again.

'The world's asleep,' Moomintroll thought. 'It's only I who am awake and sleepless. It's only I who have to wander and wander, day after day and week upon week, until I too become a snowdrift that no one will even know about.'

Just then the wood opened out, and before him stretched another valley. On the other side of it he saw the Lonely Mountains. They rolled away southwards in wave upon wave, and never had they looked more lonely.

Only now Moomintroll began to feel the cold. The evening darkness came crawling out of the clefts and climbed slowly up towards the frozen ridges. Up there the snow was gleaming like bared fangs against the black mountain; white and black, and loneliness everywhere.

'Somewhere on the other side of it all is Snufkin,' Moomintroll said to himself. 'He's sitting somewhere in the sun, peeling an orange. If I only knew that he knew that I'm climbing these mountains for his sake, then I could do it. But all alone I'll never manage it.'

And Moomintroll turned around and slowly plodded back in his own tracks.

'I'll wind all the clocks,' he thought. 'Perhaps that makes the spring come a tiny bit earlier. And someone might wake up if I happen to break some big thing.'

But he knew in his heart that no one would wake up.

Then something happened. A small track went scuttling across Moomintroll's own track. He stopped and stood looking at it for a long time. Something alive had padded through the wood, perhaps no more than half an hour ago. It couldn't have gone far. It had gone towards the valley and must have been smaller than he himself. Its paws had hardly sunk into the snow at all.

Moomintroll felt all hot inside, from the tip of his tail to the tops of his ears.

'Wait!' he shouted. 'Don't leave me alone!' He whimpered a little as he went stumbling along again through the snow, and all of a sudden he felt a great terror of the darkness and the loneliness. His fright must have hidden itself somewhere all the time since he awoke in the sleeping house, but this was the first time he dared to feel really afraid.

Now he didn't shout any more, because he thought how horrible it would be if nobody answered him. He didn't even dare to lift his snout from the track that was hardly visible in the dark. He just crawled and stumbled along, and whimpered softly to himself.

And then he caught sight of the light.

It was quite small, and yet it filled all the wood with a mild, red glow.

Moomintroll calmed down. He forgot the track and continued slowly on his way, looking towards the light. Until at last he saw that it was an ordinary candle, thrust steadily upright in the snow. Around it stood a small sugar-loaf of a house, built of round snowballs. They looked transparent and slightly orange-yellow, like the shade of the night-lamp at home.

On the other side of the lamp someone had dug herself a cosy hole, someone who lay looking up at the serene winter sky and whistling very softly to herself.

'What song is that?' asked Moomintroll.

'It's a song of myself,' someone answered from the pit.

'A song of Too-ticky who built a snow lantern, but the refrain is about wholly other things.'

'I see,' Moomintroll said and seated himself in the snow.

'No, you don't,' replied Too-ticky genially and rose up enough to show her red and white sweater. 'Because the refrain is about the things one can't understand. I'm thinking about the aurora borealis. You can't tell if it really does exist or if it just looks like existing. All things are so very uncertain, and that's exactly what makes me feel reassured.'

She lay down in the snow again and continued looking up at the sky. It was quite black by now.

Moomintroll also put up his snout and looked at the sparkling northern lights that probably no Moomin had ever seen before him. They were white and blue and a little green, and they draped the sky in long, fluttering curtains.

'I think it exists,' he said.

Too-ticky did not reply. She crawled up to the snow lantern and lifted out her candle.

'We'll take this home,' she said. 'Before the Groke comes and sits down on it.'

Moomintroll nodded gravely. He had seen the Groke once. An August night long ago. Cold and grey like a lump of ice she had squatted in the shadows of the lilac bushes and just looked at him. But what a look! And when she slunk away the ground was frosted white where she had sat.

For a moment Moomintroll wondered whether winter itself wasn't something that ten thousand Grokes had made by squatting on the ground. But he decided to take

up this matter later on when he knew Too-ticky a little better.

While they found their way back the valley seemed lighter, and Moomintroll saw that the moon was up.

The Moominhouse stood by itself, asleep, on the other side of the bridge. But here Too-ticky turned westward and made a short cut through the bare fruit orchard.

'There were a lot of apples here last fall,' Moomintroll remarked sociably.

'But now here's a lot of snow,' replied Too-ticky distantly, without stopping.

They came down to the shore. The sea was one single, vast darkness. They walked cautiously out on the narrow landing stage that led to the Moomin family's bathing-house.

'I used to dive from here,' Moomintroll whispered very softly and looked at the yellowed and broken reeds that stuck out of the ice. 'The sea was so warm, and I swam nine strokes under water.'

Too-ticky opened the door to the bathing-house. She

went in first and set the candle on the round table that Moominpappa had found floating in the sea long ago.

Everything was quite the same as usual in the old octagonal bathing-house. The knot-holes in the yellowed board walls, the small green and red window-panes, the narrow benches, and the cupboard that held the bath-gowns and the slightly air-leaking rubber Hemulen.

Everything was exactly as in summer. But still the room had changed in some mysterious way.

Too-ticky took off her cap, and it climbed straight up the wall and hung itself on a peg.

'I'd like to have a cap like that,' said Moomintroll.

'You don't need any,' said Too-ticky. 'You can always wiggle your ears and keep warm that way. But you've got cold paws.'

And over the floor two woollen socks came waddling and laid themselves down before Moomintroll.

At the same time a fire was kindled in the three-legged iron stove in the far corner, and someone started cauti-ously to play the flute under the table.

'He's shy,' Too-ticky explained. 'That's why he plays under the table.'

27

'But why doesn't he even show himself?' asked Moomintroll.

'They're all so shy that they've gone invisible,' Tooticky replied. 'They're eight very small shrews who share this house with me.'

'This is Daddy's bathing-house,' Moomintroll said.

Too-ticky gave him a serious look. 'You may be right, and you may be wrong,' she said. 'In the summer it belonged to a daddy. In winter it belongs to Too-ticky.'

A pot started to boil on the stove. The lid was lifted off, and a spoon stirred the soup. Another spoon put in a pinch of salt and tidily returned it to the window-sill.

Outside the cold sharpened towards the night, and the moonlight was reflected in all the green and red panes.

'Tell me about the snow,' Moomintroll said and seated himself in Moominpappa's sun-bleached garden chair. 'I don't understand it.'

'I don't either,' said Too-ticky. 'You believe it's cold, but if you build yourself a snowhouse it's warm. You think it's white, but at times it looks pink, and another time it's blue. It can be softer than anything, and then again harder than stone. Nothing is certain.'

A plate of fish-soup came carefully gliding through the air and put itself on the table before Moomintroll.

'Where have your shrews learned to fly?' he asked.

'Well,' said Too-ticky. 'Better not ask people about everything. They might like to keep their secrets to themselves. Don't you worry about the shrews, nor about the snow.'

Moomintroll drank his soup.

He looked at the cupboard in the corner and thought of how nice it was to know that his own old bath-gown

was hanging inside it. That something certain and cosy still remained in the middle of all the new and worrying things. He knew that his bath-gown was blue, and that its hanger was missing and there was probably a pair of sun-glasses in the left pocket.

After a while he said: 'That's where we used to keep our bath-gowns. Mother's is hanging farthest in from the door.'

Too-ticky reached out her paw and caught a sandwich. 'Thanks,' she said. 'You must never open that cupboard. You'll have to promise me.'

'I won't promise anything,' Moomintroll said surlily, looking down into his soup-plate.

All of a sudden he found that it was the most important thing in the world to open that door and to see for himself whether the bath-gown was still there.

The fire was going nicely. It roared in the stove-pipe. The bathing-house was warm and pleasant, and under the table the flute took up its lonely tune.

Invisible paws carried the empty plates away. The candle burned down, and the wick drowned in a lake of grease. Now the only light came from the red eye of the stove and the pattern of red and green moonshine squares on the floor.

'I'm sleeping at home tonight,' Moomintroll said sternly.

'Fine,' replied Too-ticky. 'Moon hasn't gone down yet, so you'll find your way easily.'

The door glided open of itself, and Moomintroll stepped out on the snowy planks.

'Never mind,' he said. 'Anyway my blue bath-gown's in the cupboard. Thanks for the soup.'

The door glided shut, and all around him was nothing but silence and moonlight.

He looked quickly out over the ice and thought he could see the big, clumsy Groke shuffling along somewhere near the horizon.

He imagined her waiting behind the boulders on the shore. And as he passed through the wood her shadow was silently creeping behind every tree-trunk. The Groke who sat down on every light and bleached every colour.

Finally Moomintroll came home to his sleeping house. Slowly he climbed the enormous snowdrift on the northern side and crawled up to the hatch in the roof.

The air inside was warm and Moomin-smelling, and the chandelier jingled in recognition when he padded over the floor. Moomintroll lifted the mattress from his bed and laid it on Moominmamma's bed-mat. She sighed a little in her sleep and mumbled something he couldn't understand. Then she laughed to herself and rolled a little nearer to the wall.

'I don't belong here any more,' Moomintroll thought. 'Nor there. I don't even know what's waking and what's a dream.' And then in an instant he was asleep, and summer lilacs covered him in their friendly green shadow.

*

Little My lay in her frayed sleeping-bag, feeling very vexed. A wind had sprung up in the evening and blew straight into the cave. The wet cardboard box had burst in three different places, and most of the stuffing was confusedly blowing about from corner to corner in the cave.

'Hello, old sister,' Little My shouted, and knocked the

Mymble in the back. But the Mymble slept. She didn't even move.

'I'm growing angry,' said Little My. 'When, for once, one could've had some use for a sister.'

She kicked herself free from the sleeping-bag. Then she crawled to the opening and looked out in the cold night with some delight.

'I'll show you all,' Little My muttered grimly and coasted down the slope.

The shore was lonelier than the end of the world (if indeed anybody has been there). With low whispers the snow was sweeping its large fans over the ice. Everything was dark, because the moon had set.

'Here we go,' said Little My and spread her skirts in the evil northern wind. She started to slide along between the snow-spots, swerving left and right, spacing her legs with the secure poise you usually have if you are a My.

The candle in the bathing-house had burned down long ago when Little My passed. She could only see the pointed roof outlined against the night sky. But she didn't think for a moment: 'There's our old bathing-house.' She sniffed the sharp and dangerous smells of winter and stopped by the shore to listen. The wolves were howling, far, far away in the Lonely Mountains.

'Makes the blood curdle,' Little My murmured, grinning to herself in the dark. Her nose told her that there was a path here that led to the Moomin valley and to the house where one could find some warm quilts and possibly even a new sleeping-bag. She dashed over the shore and straight in among the trees.

She was so small that her feet made no tracks at all in the snow.

CHAPTER 3

The Great Cold

ALL the clocks were running again. Moomintroll felt
less lonely after he had wound them up. As time was lost
anyway, he set them at different hours. Perhaps one of
them would be right, he thought.

Every so often they struck, and now and then the
alarm clock went off. It comforted him. But he could
never forget the one terrible thing – that the sun didn't
rise any longer. Yes, it's true; morning after morning
broke in a kind of grey twilight and melted back again
into the long winter night – but the sun never showed
himself. He was lost, simply lost, perhaps he had rolled
out into space. At first Moomintroll refused to believe it.
He waited a long time.

Every day he went down to the shore and sat there to
wait, with his snout to the south-east. But nothing
happened. Then he went home again and closed the
hatch in the roof and lit a row of candles on the drawing-
room mantelpiece.

The Dweller Under the Sink had still not come out to eat but was probably living a secret and important life by himself.

The Groke sauntered about on the ice, deep in her own thoughts that no one would ever learn, and in the cupboard of the bathing-house something dangerous was lurking among the gowns. Whatever can one do about such things?

Such things just *are*, but one never knows why, and one feels hopelessly apart.

Moomintroll found a large box of paper transfers in the attic and lapsed into longing admiration of their summerish beauty. They were pictures of flowers and sunrises and little carts with gaudy wheels, glossy and peaceful pictures that reminded him of the world he had lost.

First he spread them out on the drawing-room floor. Then he hit upon pasting them on the walls. He pasted slowly and carefully to make the job last, and the brightest pictures he pasted above his sleeping Mamma.

Moomintroll had pasted along all the way to the looking-glass before he noticed that the silver tray had disappeared. It had always hung to the right of the looking-glass in a red, cross-stitched tray hanger, and now there was only the hanger, and a dark oval on the wallpaper.

He felt very upset because he knew that Moomin-mamma loved the tray. It was a family treasure that no one was allowed to use, and it used to be the only thing that was polished for Midsummer.

Distractedly, Moomintroll hunted everywhere. He found no tray. But he discovered that several other

things were missing also, such as pillows and quilts, flour and sugar, and a kettle. Even the egg-cosy with the rose embroidery.

Moomintroll felt deeply offended, as he regarded himself as responsible on behalf of the sleeping family. At first he suspected the Dweller Under the Sink. He also thought of the Groke and of the mystery of the bathing-house cupboard. But the guilty one could indeed be anybody. The winter probably was peopled with strange creatures who acted mysteriously and freakishly.

'I must ask Too-ticky,' thought Moomintroll. 'True, I intended to punish the sun by staying at home until he comes back. But this is important.'

*

When Moomintroll stepped out in the grey twilight, a strange white horse was standing by the verandah, staring at him with luminous eyes. He cautiously approached and greeted it, but the horse didn't move.

Moomintroll now saw that it was made of snow. Its

tail was the broom from the woodshed, and its eyes were
small mirrors. He could see his own picture in the mirror
eyes, and this frightened him a little. So he made a detour by the bare jasmine bushes.

'If there only were a single soul here that I knew of
old,' Moomintroll thought. 'Somebody who wouldn't be
mysterious, just quite ordinary. Somebody who had also
awakened and didn't feel at home. Then one could say:
"Hello! Terribly cold, isn't it? Snow's a silly thing,
what? Have you seen the jasmine bushes? Remember
last summer, when . . .?"

'Or things like that.'

Too-ticky sat on the bridge parapet, singing.

'I'm Too-ticky, and I've made a horse,'
she sang.

> A wild, white horse that goes a-gallop
> Stamping o'er the ice into the night,
> A white and solemn horse that goes a-gallop
> Carrying the Great Cold upon his back.

Then followed the refrain.

'How do you mean?' asked Moomintroll.

'I mean that we'll spill river water over him tonight,' Too-ticky said. 'Then he'll freeze during the night and become all ice. And when the Great Cold comes he'll gallop off and never return any more.'

Moomintroll was silent.

Then he said: 'Somebody's carrying off things from Daddy's house.'

'That's nice, isn't it,' replied Too-ticky cheerfully. 'You've got too many things about you. As well as things you remember, and things you're dreaming about.'

And she started the second stanza.

Moomintroll turned about and went away. 'She doesn't understand me,' he thought. Behind him the exultant chant went on.

'Sing all you want,' Moomintroll muttered, angry to the point of crying. 'Sing about your horrible winter with

black ice and unfriendly snow-horses, and people who never appear but only hide and are queer!'

He tramped up the slope, he kicked at the snow, his tears froze on his snout, and suddenly he started to sing his own song.

He sang it at the top of his voice, so that Too-ticky would hear it and be put out.

This was Moomintroll's angry summer song:

Listen, winter creatures, who have sneaked the sun away,

39

Who are hiding in the dark and making all the valley
  grey:
I am utterly alone, and I'm tired to the bone,
And I'm sick enough of snowdrifts just to lay me down
  and groan.
I want my blue verandah and the glitter of the sea
And I tell you one and all that your winter's not for
  me!

'Just you wait until my sun's coming back to look at
you, and then you'll look silly, all of you,' Moomintroll
shouted and didn't even care about his rhymes any more.

Because then I'll dance on a sunflower disk
And lie on my stomach in the warm sand
And keep my window open all the day
On the garden and bumblebees
And on the sky-blue sky
And my own great
Orange-yellow
SUN!

The silence was oppressive when Moomintroll finished his song of defiance.

He stood listening for a while, but nobody opposed
him.

'Something's bound to happen,' he thought with a
tremble. And something did happen.

High up, from near the top of the hill, something came
coasting along. It shot downwards in a plume of glittering snow, and it shouted: 'Stand aside! Keep clear!'

Moomintroll could only stare.

Straight towards him rushed the silver tray, and on it
sat the missing egg-cosy. 'Too-ticky must have poured

river-water on them,' Moomintroll had time to reflect. 'And now they're alive and galloping away and won't ever return any more . . .'

The collision came. Moomintroll was thrown deep into the snow, and even under the surface he could hear Too-ticky's laughter.

There was also another laugh, a laugh that could belong only to one person in the whole world.

'Little My!' shouted Moomintroll with his mouth full of snow. He clambered to his feet, beside himself with happiness and expectation.

Yes, there she was sitting in the snow. She had cut holes for her head and arms in the tea-cosy, and an embroidered rose adorned the middle of her stomach.

'Little My!' cried Moomintroll once again. 'Oh, you can't even guess . . . It's been so strange, so lonely . . . Remember last summer when . . .?'

'But now it's winter,' said Little My and fished for the silver tray in the snow. 'We took a good jump, didn't we?'

'I woke up and couldn't go to sleep again,' Moomintroll told her. 'The door had stuck, and the sun was lost, and not even the Dweller Under the Sink would . . .'

'Quite, quite,' Little My said cheerfully. 'So then you

started pasting transfers on the walls. You're the same old Moomintroll. Now I wonder if it would speed up this tray a bit to rub it with candle-grease?'

'That's an idea,' said Too-ticky.

'I suppose I'll get quite a kick out of it on the ice,' said Little My. 'If one can find something for a sail in the Moominhouse.'

Moomintroll looked at them and thought a while.

Then he said quietly: 'You can always borrow my sun tent.'

*

The same afternoon Too-ticky felt in her nose that the Great Cold was on its way. She poured river water over the horse and carried armfuls of wood to the bathing-house.

'Keep inside today, because she'll be coming,' Too-ticky said.

The invisible shrews nodded, and an agreeing rustle was heard from the cupboard. Too-ticky went out to warn the others.

'Take it easy,' said Little My. 'I'll be coming in all right when I feel the pinch in my toes. And I can always throw some straw over the Mymble.' My steered her silver tray out on the ice.

Too-ticky continued her way towards the valley. On the path she met the squirrel with the marvellous tail. 'Keep at home tonight, because the Great Cold is coming,' said Too-ticky.

'Yes,' said the squirrel. 'You haven't seen a spruce cone I left here somewhere?'

'I haven't,' said Too-ticky. 'But promise that you

won't forget what I told you. Stay at home after twilight. It's important.'

The squirrel nodded absentmindedly.

Too-ticky went on to the Moominhouse and climbed the rope ladder that Moomintroll had hung out. She opened the hatch and called to him.

Moomintroll was darning the family's bathing trunks with red cotton yarn.

'I just wanted to tell you that the Great Cold's on her way,' Too-ticky said.

'A still greater one?' asked Moomintroll. 'How big do they grow?'

'This is the most dangerous of them all,' said Too-ticky. 'And she'll come in the afternoon, when the sky changes to green, straight in from the sea.'

'It's a she then?' asked Moomintroll.

'Yes, and very beautiful,' said Too-ticky. 'But if you look her in the face you'll be frozen to ice. You'll be hard like a biscuit and not even crumble. That's why you'd better keep at home tonight.'

Too-ticky crawled back out on the roof. Moomintroll went down in the cellar and filled more peat into the central-heating stove. He also spread some carpets over the sleeping family.

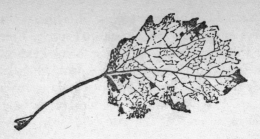

Then he wound the clocks and went out. He felt like having some company when the Lady of the Cold would make her visit.

*

As Moomintroll reached the bathing-house, the sky was already paler and greener than before. The wind had gone to sleep, and the dead reeds sprouted stiff and immobile from the ice by the shore.

He listened, and he thought that he could hear a very low, deep and softly humming tone in the silence itself. Perhaps it came from the ice that was freezing itself deeper and deeper down in the sea.

The bathing-house felt well warmed, and on the table stood Moominmamma's blue teapot.

He sat down in the garden chair and asked: 'When is she coming?'

'Quite soon now,' said Too-ticky. 'But don't worry.'

'Well, the Lady of the Cold doesn't worry me any,' said Moomintroll. 'I'm worried by *the others*. Those that I don't know anything about. Like the Dweller Under the Sink. And that one in the cupboard. Or the Groke that only looks at you and never says a word.'

Too-ticky rubbed her nose and thought. 'Well, it's like

this,' she said. 'There are such a lot of things that have no place in summer and autumn and spring. Everything that's a little shy and a little rum. Some kinds of night animals and people that don't fit in with others and that nobody really believes in. They keep out of the way all the year. And then when everything's quiet and white and the nights are long and most people are asleep – then they appear.'

'Do *you* know them?' asked Moomintroll.

'Some of them,' replied Too-ticky. 'The Dweller Under the Sink, for instance, quite well. But I believe that he wants to lead a secret life, so I can't introduce you to each other.'

Moomintroll kicked at the table leg and sighed. 'I see, I see,' he replied. 'But I don't want to lead a secret life. Here one comes stumbling into something altogether new and strange, and not a soul even asking one in what kind of a world one has lived before. Not even Little My wants to talk about the *real* world.'

'And how does one tell which one is the real one?' said Too-ticky with her nose pressed against a pane. 'Here she is.'

The door was pushed open, and Little My sent the silver tray clattering in along the floor.

'The sail's not bad,' she said. 'But what I really need now is a muff. Your Mamma's eggwarmer'll never do, no matter where I cut the holes. Already it looked like something one wouldn't even have the cheek to give away to a displaced hedgehog.'*

* A displaced hedgehog is a hedgehog that has been removed from its home against its will and not even had the time to pack its toothbrush – *Author's Note.*

'I can see that,' replied Moomintroll with a bleak look at the eggwarmer.

Little My threw it on the floor, and it was immediately tidied off into the stove by an invisible shrew.

'Well, is she coming?' said Little My.

'I think so,' said Too-ticky quietly. 'Let's take a look outside.'

They went out on to the landing-stage and sniffed towards the sea. The evening sky was green all over, and all the world seemed to be made of thin glass. All was silent, nothing stirred, and slender stars were shining everywhere and twinkling in the ice. It was terribly cold.

'Yes, she's on her way,' said Too-ticky. 'We'd better go inside.'

The shrew stopped playing under the table.

Far out on the ice came the Lady of the Cold. She was pure white, like the candles, but if one looked at her through the right pane she became red, and seen through the left one she was pale green.

Suddenly Moomintroll felt the pane become so cold that it hurt, and he drew back his snout in rather a fright.

They sat down by the stove and waited.

'Don't look,' said Too-ticky.

'Hello, here's someone crawling into my lap,' cried
Little My surprisedly and looked down at her empty
skirt.

'It's my shrews,' said Too-ticky. 'They're scared. Sit
still, and they'll go away soon.'

Now the Lady of the Cold was walking past the
bathing-house. Perhaps she did cast an eye through the
window, because an icy draught suddenly swept through
the room and darkened the red-hot stove for a moment.
Then it was over. Feeling a little embarrassed, the invisible shrews jumped down from Little My's lap, and
everybody rushed to the window and looked out.

The Lady of the Cold was standing by the reeds. Her
back was turned, and she was bending down over the
snow.

'It's the squirrel,' said Too-ticky. 'He's forgotten to
keep at home.'

The Lady of the Cold turned her beautiful face towards the squirrel and distractedly scratched him behind one ear. Bewitched, he stared back at her, straight into her cold blue eyes. The Lady of the Cold smiled and continued on her way.

But she left the foolish little squirrel lying stiff and numb with all his paws in the air.

'Too bad,' said Too-ticky grimly and pulled her cap over her ears. She opened the door, and a cloud of white snow-fog came whirling in. She darted out, and in a moment she slipped back in again and laid the squirrel on the table.

The invisible shrews came running with hot water and rolled the squirrel in a warmed towel. But his little legs sprouted just as sadly and stiffly in the air, and he did not move a whisker.

'He's quite dead,' said Little My matter-of-factly.

'At least he saw something beautiful before he died,' said Moomintroll in a trembling voice.

'Oh, well,' said Little My. 'In any case he's forgotten it by now. And I'm going to make myself a sweet little muff out of his tail.'

'But you can't!' Moomintroll cried, very upset. 'He must have his tail with him in the grave. Because he has to be buried, hasn't he, Too-ticky?'

'Mphm,' replied Too-ticky. 'It's very hard to tell if

people take any pleasure in their tails when they're dead.'

'Please,' said Moomintroll. 'Don't talk about him being dead all the time. It's so sad.'

'When one's dead, then one's dead,' said Too-ticky kindly. 'This squirrel will become earth all in his time. And still later on there'll grow trees from him, with new squirrels skipping about in them. Do you think that's so very sad?'*

'Perhaps not,' said Moomintroll, and blew his snout. 'But in any case he's going to be buried tomorrow, and his tail too, and we'll have a nice and very proper funeral.'

*

The following day it was very cold in the bathing-house. The fire was lighted in the stove, but evidently the invisible shrews were tired. The coffee pot that Moomintroll had brought from home had a thin layer of ice under the lid.

Moomintroll wouldn't take any coffee, out of consideration for the dead squirrel. 'You'll have to give me my bath-gown,' he said solemnly. 'Mother's told me that funerals are always cold.'

'Turn your back and count ten,' said Too-ticky.

Moomintroll turned towards the window and counted. At eight Too-ticky shut the cupboard door and gave him his blue gown.

'Oh, you remembered that mine was the blue one,' Moomintroll said happily. He stuck his paws in the

* In case the reader feels like having a cry, please take a quick look at page 126. *Author's Note*.

pockets at once but found no sun-glasses there, only a little sand and a perfectly round and smooth, white pebble.

He closed his paw around the pebble. Its roundness held all the security of summer. He could even imagine that it was still a little warm from lying in the sun.

'You look as if you were at the wrong party,' said Little My.

Moomintroll didn't look at her.

'Are you coming to the funeral or not?' he asked in a dignified manner.

'Of course we're coming,' said Too-ticky. 'He was a nice squirrel in his way.'

'Especially the tail,' Little My said.

They wrapped the squirrel in an old bathing-cap and stepped out into the bitter cold.

The snow crunched under their paws, and their breaths became clouds of white smoke. Moomintroll soon felt his snout stiffen so that it was impossible to wrinkle it.

'Tough going, this,' Little My said happily and skipped along over the frozen shore.

'Can't you slow up a bit,' asked Moomintroll. 'This *is* a funeral.'

He was able to draw only very short breaths of the icy air.

'I never knew you had any eyebrows at all,' said Little My interestedly. 'Now they're all white and you look more confused than ever.'

'That's rime,' said Too-ticky sternly. 'And keep quiet now, because neither you nor I know anything about funerals.'

Moomintroll cheered up. He carried the squirrel up to the house and laid it down before the snow-horse.

Then he went up the rope-ladder and down into the warm, peaceful drawing-room where everybody lay asleep.

He searched all the drawers. He ransacked every place, but he didn't find what he needed.

He went to his Mother's bed and whispered a question in her ear. She sighed and turned around. Moomintroll repeated his whisper.

Then Moominmamma answered, from the depths of her womanly understanding of all that preserves tradition: 'Black bands ... they're in my cupboard ... top shelf ... to the right...' And she sank back into her winter sleep again.

But Moomintroll took out the ladder from under the staircase and climbed up to the top shelf of the cupboard.

There he found the box with all those superfluous things that can sometimes be absolutely necessary: black bands for mourning, golden bands for great celebrations, and the key to the house, and the champagne whisk, and the tube of porcelain glue, and spare brass knobs for the bedposts among other things.

When Moomintroll came out again he had a black bow on his tail. He also made fast a little black bow on Too-ticky's cap.

But Little My refused blankly to be decorated. 'If I feel sorry I needn't show it with a bow,' she said.

'*If* you feel sorry, that is,' said Moomintroll. 'But you don't.'

'No,' said Little My. 'I can't. I'm always either glad or angry. Would it help the squirrel if I were sorry? No. But if I'm angry at the Lady of the Cold, I might bite her leg some time. And then perhaps she'll take care not to scratch other little squirrels behind their ears just because they're sweet and fluffy.'

'There's something in that,' said Too-ticky. 'But

Moomintroll's also right, however that's possible. And what do we do now?'

'Now I'm going to dig a hole in the ground,' said Moomintroll. 'This is a nice spot, there are a lot of marguerites here in summer.'

'But dearest,' said Too-ticky sadly. 'The ground's frozen stone hard. You couldn't bury even a grasshopper in it.'

Moomintroll looked helplessly at her without replying. No one said a word. And at that moment the snow-horse lowered its head and cautiously sniffed at the squirrel. It looked questioningly at Moomintroll with its mirror eyes, and its broom-tail moved slightly.

At the same time the invisible shrew struck up a sad tune on his flute. Moomintroll nodded gratefully.

Then the snow-horse lifted the squirrel on his back, tail and bathing-cap and all, and everybody started to walk back to the shore.

And Too-ticky sang this about the squirrel:

> There was a little squirrel,
> A very small squirrel.
> He wasn't very clever
> But his fur was nice and warm.
> Now he is cold, quite cold.
> And all his legs are numb.
> But still he is the squirrel
> With the marvellous tail.

When the horse felt hard ice under his hooves, he tossed his head and his eyes lighted up; and suddenly he cut a caper and galloped off.

The invisible shrew changed to a fast and lively tune. Farther and farther away galloped the snow-horse with the squirrel on his back. Finally he was just a speck on the horizon.

'I wonder if this went off right?' said Moomintroll worriedly.

'It couldn't have been better,' said Too-ticky.

'Well, it could,' said Little My. 'If only I had got the nice tail for a muff.'

CHAPTER 4

The lonely and the rum

A FEW days after the squirrel's funeral Moomintroll noticed that somebody had stolen peat from the wood-shed.

There were broad tracks in the snow outside, just as if heavy sacks had been lugged off.

'It can't be My,' thought Moomintroll. 'She's much too small. And Too-ticky only takes what she needs. It must be the Groke.'

He followed the trail with bristling neck fluff. There was no one else to keep watch over the family's fuel, and this was a matter of honour.

The trail ended on the top of the hill behind the cave.

There lay the peat sacks. They were piled up to make part of a bonfire, and on top of them rested the family's garden sofa that had lost one of its legs in August.

'That sofa's going to look fine,' said Too-ticky, stepping out from behind the bonfire. 'It's old and dry as dust.'

'Certainly,' said Moomintroll. 'It's been a long time in the family. We could have repaired it.'

'Or made a new one,' said Too-ticky. 'Would you like to hear the song about Too-ticky who made a great winter bonfire?'

'By all means,' replied Moomintroll, good-naturedly.

And Too-ticky started at once to stamp around slowly in the snow, while she sang as follows:

Here come the dumb,
The lonely and the rum,
The wild and the quiet.
Thud goes the drum.

Crackle goes the bonfire
Glowing in the white snow,
Swish go the tails,
Swinging through the light snow.
Thud goes the drumming
In the black, black night.

'I've got enough of your snow and night,' cried the Moomintroll. 'No, I won't hear the refrain. I'm cold! I'm lonely! I want the sun back again!'

'But that's exactly why we burn up the great winter

bonfire tonight,' said Too-ticky. 'You'll get your sun back tomorrow.'

'My sun,' repeated Moomintroll in a trembling voice.

Too-ticky nodded and rubbed her nose.

Moomintroll was silent a long while.

Then he cautiously asked: 'Do you think she'd notice if the garden sofa were there or not?'

'Now listen,' replied Too-ticky sternly. 'This bonfire is a thousand years older than your garden sofa. You ought to feel honoured by its being good enough to be laid on top.'

And Moomintroll said no more. 'I'll have to explain that to the family,' he thought. 'And perhaps there'll be new driftwood and a new sofa on the shore after the spring gales.'

The pyre was growing. Dried-up tree-trunks were being lugged up the hillside, as well as rotten stubs, old casks and battens that people seemed to have found on the shore. But the people themselves never came into view. Moomintroll had a feeling that the hill was thronged with them, but he never caught sight of anybody.

Little My came along, trailing her cardboard box in the snow. 'I won't need it now,' she said. 'The silver tray's much better. And my sister seems to like sleeping in the drawing-room carpet. When are we going to light the fire.'

'At moonrise,' said Too-ticky.

Moomintroll felt greatly excited all evening. He padded from one room to the next and lit more candles than usual. Now and again he stood still, listening to the even breathing of the sleepers and to the light snapping in the walls as the cold sharpened.

He felt certain that all the mysterious people would come out of their holes and dens tonight, all the light-shy and unreal that Too-ticky had talked about. They'd come padding up to the great bonfire that all the small beasts had lighted to make the dark and the cold go away. And now *he* would see them.

Moomintroll lit the oil-lamp and went up to the attic.

He opened the hatch. The moon had not yet risen, but

the valley was bleakly lighted by the aurora borealis. Down by the bridge a file of torches was moving along, surrounded by leaping shadows. They were on their way to the seashore and the hilltop.

Moomintroll climbed cautiously down with the lighted lamp in his hand. The garden and the wood were filled with flickering lights and whispers, and all tracks were leading towards the hill.

When he reached the shore the moon was already high over the ice, chalk-blue and terribly remote. Something moved beside Moomintroll, and he looked down into Little My's ferociously gleaming eyes.

'It's going to be quite a fire,' she laughed. 'Make all the moonshine look silly.'

They looked towards the hilltop at the same time and saw a yellow flame rising against the sky. Too-ticky had lit the bonfire.

It wrapped itself in flames at once, from ground to top, it gave a roar like a lion and threw its reflection straight down on the black ice. A lonely little tune came running past Moomintroll: it was the invisible shrew who was a little late for the winter ritual.

Small and great shadows were solemnly skipping round the fire on the hilltop. Tails were beginning to thud on drums.

'Good-bye to your garden sofa,' said Little My.

'I've never needed it,' Moomintroll replied, impatiently. He stumbled up the icy slope. It was glittering in the firelight. The snow was melting from the heat, and the warm water wet his paws.

'The sun's coming back again,' Moomintroll thought in great excitement. 'No darkness, no loneliness any more. Once again I'll sit in the sun on the verandah and feel my back warming . . .'

Now he was up on the top. The air was hot around the fire. The invisible shrew was blowing another and wilder tune.

But the dancing shadows were already gliding away, and the drums were thudding on the other side of the fire.

'Why did they go away?' asked Moomintroll.

Too-ticky looked at him with her calm, blue eyes. Still, he wasn't quite sure that she really did see him. She was looking into her own private winter world that had followed its own strange rules year after year, while he had lain sleeping in the warm Moominhouse.

'Where's he that lives in the bathing-house cupboard?' Moomintroll asked.

'What did you say?' said Too-ticky, absentmindedly.

'I'd like to meet him that lives in the bathing-house cupboard!' repeated Moomintroll.

'Oh, but he's not allowed to come out,' said Too-ticky. 'You can't tell what such a one would find in his head to do.'

A herd of small creatures with spindly legs came blowing like a wisp of smoke over the ice. Someone with silvered horns walked stamping past Moomintroll and over the fire flapped something black with large wings, and disappeared northwards. But everything happened a little too quickly, and Moomintroll never found time to introduce himself.

'Please, Too-ticky,' he asked, pulling at her sweater.

She said kindly: 'Well, there's the Dweller Under the Sink.'

He was a rather small one, with bushy eyebrows. He sat by himself, looking into the fire.

Moomintroll sat down beside him and said: 'I hope those biscuits weren't too old?'

The little beast looked at him but didn't reply.

'May I compliment you on your exceptionally bushy eyebrows?' Moomintroll continued politely.

To this the beast with the eyebrows replied: 'Shadaff oomoo.'

'Eh?' asked Moomintroll, surprisedly.

'Radamsah,' said the little beast fretfully.

'He has a language all his own, and now he believes that you've hurt him,' Too-ticky explained.

'But that wasn't my intention at all,' said Moomintroll anxiously. 'Radamsah, radamsah,' he added imploringly.

This seemed to make the beast with the eyebrows really overcome by rage. He rose in great haste and disappeared.

'Dear me, what shall I do?' said Moomintroll. 'Now he'll live under our sink for a whole year more without knowing that I just wanted to be friends with him.'

'Such things happen,' said Too-ticky.

The garden sofa crumbled to pieces in a shower of sparks.

Nearly all the flames had died down by now, but great embers were still smouldering, and the water was bubbling in the crevices. But the shrew suddenly stopped playing, and everybody looked out towards the ice.

The Groke was sitting there. Her round little eyes reflected the glow, but otherwise she was just a large shapeless greyness. She had grown a lot since August.

The drums ceased while the Groke came shuffling up the hillside. She went straight to the fire. And without saying a word she sat down on it.

There was a sharp hissing sound, and the hilltop was wrapped in mist. When it passed away again, no embers were to be seen. Only a big grey Groke blowing snow-fog about her.

Moomintroll had fled down to the shore with many others. He found Too-ticky there also and shouted:

'What happens now? Has the Groke made the sun stay away?'

'Take it easy,' replied Too-ticky. 'She didn't come to extinguish the fire, you see, she came to warm herself, poor creature. But everything that's warm goes cold when she sits down on it. Now she's disappointed once more.'

Moomintroll saw the Groke rise again and sniff at the frosted charcoal. She then went over to his oil-lamp that was still alight in the snow. He saw it go out.

The Groke remained immobile for a moment. The hill was empty, everybody had left. Then she glided down to the ice again and back into the dark, as she had come, alone.

Moomintroll went home.

Before he went to bed he cautiously pulled Moominmamma's ear and told her: 'It wasn't a very funny party.'

'Really, dear me,' mumbled Moominmamma in her sleep. 'Perhaps next time . . .'

But under the sink sat the beast with the bushy eyebrows, grumbling to himself.

'Radamsah!' he said crossly. 'Radamsah!' and shrugged his shoulders violently. Probably no one in the whole valley would have understood what he was saying.

*

Too-ticky was sitting under the ice with her fishing-rod. She liked the sea's habit of sinking a bit now and then. At those times she could easily climb down through a hole by the landing-stage and seat herself on a boulder to fish. Then one had a nice green ceiling of ice overhead, and the sea at one's feet.

A black floor and a green ceiling, both stretching away into the darkness.

Beside Too-ticky lay four small fish. One more, and she'd have her soup.

Suddenly she heard impatient steps coming nearer on the landing-stage. Up there Moomintroll rapped at the bathing-house door. He waited a moment and knocked again.

'Ho!' shouted Too-ticky. 'I'm under the ice!'

The echo raised its head somewhere to the left of her and shouted: 'Ho!' It went sliding back and forth several times and cried: 'Under the ice!'

After a while Moomintroll's snout cautiously appeared in the opening. His ears were decorated with limp gold ribbons.

He looked at the steaming, black water and at Too-ticky's four fish.

He shivered, and said: 'Well, he didn't come.'

'Who didn't?' asked Too-ticky.

'The sun!' cried Moomintroll.

'The sun,' repeated the echo. 'Sun, sun, sun...' farther and farther off, weaker and weaker.

Too-ticky hauled on her line.

'Don't be in such a hurry,' she said. 'He's been coming on this day every year, so probably he'll do it now again. Pull up your snout so I can come out of here.'

Too-ticky clambered up to the surface and sat down on the bathing-house steps. She sniffed lightly and listened. Then she said: 'Soon now. Sit down and wait.'

Little My came skating over the ice and sat down beside them. She had tied tin lids under her shoes for better speed.

'So here we're waiting for something wonderful again,' she said. 'Not that I wouldn't like a little daylight.'

Two old crows came flapping from the wood and alighted on the roof of the bathing-house. The minutes passed.

All at once the fluff on Moomintroll's back bristled, and in great excitement he saw a red light gathering on the dusky sky just over the horizon. It thickened to a narrow, red sliver of fire that threw long, red rays of light along the ice.

'There he is!' cried Moomintroll.

He lifted Little My in his arms and kissed her smack on the nose.

'Golly, what a fuss,' said Little My. 'What's all this to make such a noise about?'

'Of course!' cried Moomintroll. 'Spring! Warmth! Everybody'll wake up! How splendid.'

He took the four fish and threw them high in the air. He stood on his head. He had never felt so happy in his life.

And then the ice became dark again.

The crows took off and went slowly flapping over the shore. Too-ticky gathered up her fishes, and the little red strip had hidden itself under the horizon.

'Did he change his mind?' Moomintroll asked, horrified.

'No wonder after taking a peep at you,' said Little My, and skated off on her tin lids.

'He'll return tomorrow,' replied Too-ticky. 'And then he'll be a tiny bit bigger, about like a piece of cheese rind. Take it easy.'

And Too-ticky crept back under the ice to fill her soup-kettle with sea-water.

Of course she was right. It can't be done in a trice for a sun to appear in the sky. But you won't be less disappointed just because other people are right and you are not.

Moomintroll sat staring down at the ice, and suddenly he felt that he was becoming angry. It started down in his tummy like all strong feelings. He felt that somebody had pulled his leg.

And he felt a fool for having made such a noise, and tied gold ribbons about his ears. That made him angrier still.

Finally he felt that he had to do something really terrible, and forbidden, to be able to calm down again. And *at once*.

He started to his feet, ran over the landing-stage and into the bathing-house. He went straight to the cupboard and threw the door wide open.

There hung the bath-gowns. There lay the rubber Hemulen that wasn't quite air-tight. Just as they had been last summer. But on the floor a grey little thing was sitting and staring at him, very hairy and grey and snouty.

Then it came to life and whizzed past him like a draught, and disappeared. He saw its tail slide out through the chink at the bathing-house door like a piece of black string. The tuft caught for a fleeting moment but was pulled free, and then the beast was gone.

Too-ticky came in with the kettle between her paws and said: 'So you couldn't keep from opening the door?'

'There was only a sort of old rat,' Moomintroll replied surlily.

'That was no rat,' said Too-ticky. 'It was a troll. A

troll of the kind you were yourself before you became a Moomin. That was how you looked a thousand years ago.'

Moomintroll found no reply. He went home and sat down in the drawing-room to think.

After a while Little My dropped in to borrow some candles and sugar. 'I hear terrible things about you,' she said happily. 'They say you've been letting your own forefather out of the cupboard. You resemble each other, I hear.'

'Shut up, please,' said Moomintroll.

He went up to the attic and found the family album.

Page after page of dignified Moomins, most often

reproduced standing in front of porcelain stoves, or on fretworked verandahs. Not a single one of them resembled the cupboard troll.

'Must be a mistake,' Moomintroll thought. 'He can't be any relation of mine.'

He went down and looked at his sleeping Daddy. Only

the snout bore some resemblance to the troll's. But possibly, a thousand years ago . . . ?

The cut-glass chandelier started jingling. It was slowly swaying back and forth, and something was moving about inside the gauze. Something small and hairy. A long, black tail was hanging straight down among the prisms.

'There he is,' Moomintroll murmured. 'My ancestor has set himself up in the chandelier.'

But now this didn't seem so very bad. Moomintroll was getting accustomed to the bewitched time of winter,

'How are you?' he asked softly. The troll looked at him through the gauze and wiggled its ears.

'Be careful with the chandelier,' Moomintroll continued. 'It's a family piece.'

The troll tilted its head and looked intently at him, obviously trying to listen.

'Now he's going to speak,' thought Moomintroll. All at once he felt terribly afraid that his ancestor might try to tell him something. What if he spoke some foreign language, like the little beast with the eyebrows? If he became angry and said 'radamsah' or something? And then they'd perhaps never be friends afterwards.

'Hush!' whispered Moomintroll. 'Don't say anything.'

Perhaps they were related after all. And relatives who have come on a visit may stay for any length of time. If it's an ancestor he may stay for ever. Who can tell? If one weren't careful he might misunderstand one and be angry. And then the family would have to live with an angry ancestor all their lives.

'Hush!' repeated Moomintroll. 'Hush!'

The ancestor jingled the prisms slightly but said nothing.

'I'll show him about the house,' Moomintroll thought. 'That's what Mother'd have done if a relative had come on a visit.'

He took the lamp and held it before a beautiful hand-painted picture called 'Fillyjonk at window'. The troll looked at it and shrugged his shoulders.

Moomintroll went on to the plush sofa. He showed the troll all the chairs, one by one, the drawing-room mirror and the meerschaum tram, everything of beauty and value that the Moomin family possessed.

The troll looked attentively at it all but it was clear that it didn't understand the use of the things. Finally Moomintroll sighed and placed the lamp on the mantelpiece. But this caught the troll's interest very strongly.

It dropped down from the chandelier and went scuttling round the porcelain stove like a little grey bundle of rags. It stuck its head inside the shutters and sniffed at the ashes. It showed great curiosity in the embroidered cord that hung from the damper, and nosed for a long time in the cranny between stove and wall.

'It must be true then,' Moomintroll thought agitatedly. 'We *are* related. Because Mother's always told me that our forebears lived behind stoves . . .'

At that moment the alarm clock went off. Moomintroll used to have it ring at dusk because that was the time when he longed most for company.

The troll stiffened visibly, and then it whizzed inside the stove in a cloud of ashes. A moment later it started rattling the damper in no very friendly way.

Moomintroll shut off the alarm clock and listened with a thumping heart. But nothing else was to be heard.

A few specks of soot came falling down the chimney, and the damper cord was swaying.

Moomintroll went out on the roof to calm himself.

'Well, how d'you like Grandfather!' Little My shouted from her sledge-slide.

'An excellent person,' Moomintroll remarked with dignity. 'In an old family like ours people know how to behave.'

Suddenly he felt very proud of having an ancestor. And it cheered him no little to think that Little My had no pedigree at all, but rather had come into the world by chance.

*

That night Moomintroll's ancestor rearranged the house, quietly enough, but with surprising strength.

In the morning he had turned the sofa towards the porcelain stove and hung all the pictures anew. Those

that he liked least he had hung upside-down. (Or perhaps they were those that he thought best of, who knows?)

Not a single piece of furniture stood in its old place, and the alarm clock lay in the slop-pail. Indeed he had carried down a heap of old junk from the attic and piled it high around the stove.

Too-ticky came over to look. 'I believe he's done that to feel more at home,' she said and rubbed her nose. 'He's tried to build himself a nice thicket around his house. So that he can be left alone.'

'But what'll Mother say?' said Moomintroll.

Too-ticky shrugged her shoulders. 'Well, why did you have to let him out?' she said. 'In any case this troll never eats anything. Very practical for him, and for you. You'll have to think the whole matter's fun, I suppose.'

Moomintroll nodded.

He thought for a while. Then he crawled inside the thicket of broken chairs, empty boxes, fishing nets, cardboard tubes, old baskets and gardening tools. Very soon he discovered that it was a cosy kind of place.

He decided to sleep the night in a basket of wool that stood under a useless rocking-chair.

As a matter of fact he had never felt really secure in the dim-lit drawing-room with its empty windows. And to look at the sleeping family made him melancholy.

But here, in the small space between a packing case, the rocking-chair and the back of the sofa, he felt at ease and not at all lonely.

He could see a little of the blackness inside the stove, but he was careful not to disturb his ancestor and built walls around his nest as quietly as he could.

In the evening he took the lamp there with him and lay for a while listening to the ancestor's rustling in the chimney.

'Perhaps I lived like this a thousand years ago,' Moomintroll thought happily.

He half thought of shouting something up the chimney. Just a word of secret concord. But then he thought better of it, blew out his lamp and curled up deep in the wool.

CHAPTER 5

The new guests

EACH day the sun rose a little higher in the sky. Finally it had reached high enough to throw a few cautious rays into the valley. That was a most important day. It was remarkable also because a stranger arrived in the valley shortly after noon.

He was a thin little dog with a tattered woollen cap pulled deep over his ears. He said that his name was Sorry-oo, and that there was no food left in the valleys to the north. Since the Lady of the Cold had passed people had had next to nothing to eat. A desperate Hemulen was even rumoured to have bolted down his own beetle collection, but this was probably untrue. Possibly he had eaten some other Hemulen's collection, however. Anyway, lots of people were now on their way towards the Moomin valley.

Somebody had told everybody that rowan-berries and a whole cellar of jam were to be found here. But probably the jam-cellar was just a rumour too . . .

Sorry-oo sat down in the snow on his thin tail, and all his face wrinkled up at his worries.

'We live on fish-soup here,' Too-ticky said. 'I've never heard about any jam-cellar.'

Moomintroll threw a sudden look at the round snow-drift behind the woodshed.

'There it is!' said Little My. 'There are such lots of jam in it that it makes you sick just to think of it, and all the jars are dated and tied with red string.'

'I'm kind of keeping an eye on the family's things while they sleep,' Moomintroll said, and blushed a little.

'Of course you are,' mumbled Sorry-oo resignedly.

Moomintroll looked at the verandah and then at Sorry-oo's wrinkled face.

'Do you like jam?' he asked gruffly.

'I don't know,' Sorry-oo replied humbly.

Moomintroll sighed and said: 'Well. Just mind that you start with the oldest jars.'

*

A few hours later a flock of small Creep came plodding over the bridge, and a confused and complaining Filly-jonk was seen to be running to and fro in the garden. Her potted plants were frozen, she said. Somebody had eaten all her winter food. And on her way to the Moomin valley she had met an insolent Gaffsie who had told her that winter was no laughing matter, and why hadn't she prepared herself better.

At dusk there were a lot of people treading paths to the jam-cellar. Those that had a little more strength left in their legs went down to the shore and settled down in the bathing-house.

But no one was allowed in the cave. Little My said that the Mymble couldn't be disturbed.

Before the Moominhouse some of the most miserable ones were sitting and lamenting their fate, when Moomintroll appeared on the roof with his oil-lamp. 'You'd better come inside for the night,' he said. 'You never know, what with Grokes and such around.'

'I never was one for rope-ladders,' declared an old Whomper.

Moomintroll descended and started to dig a hole to the entrance door. He shovelled and scratched and worked away. Soon the hole was a long and narrow tunnel extending through the snow, but when he finally reached the wall there was no door to be found. Only a window, frozen fast like the others.

'I must have dug wrong,' Moomintroll said to himself. 'And if I dig a new tunnel perhaps I'll miss the house altogether.' So he broke the window-pane as nicely as possible, and the guests soon came crawling in after him.

'Please don't awaken the family,' said Moomintroll. 'This is Mother, and that's Father, and over there's the Snork Maiden. My ancestor sleeps in the stove. You'll have to roll yourself up in the carpets because most of the other things have been borrowed.'

The guests bowed to the sleeping family. Then they obligingly rolled themselves up in carpets and tablecloths, and the smallest ones went to sleep in caps, slippers and the like.

Many of them had a cold, and some of them were homesick. 'This is terrible,' Moomintroll thought. 'Very soon the jam-cellar'll be empty. And what shall I say when the family awakes in the spring, and all the pictures

are hanging wrong and the house is thronged with people?'

He crawled back through the tunnel to see if anybody had been left outside.

The moonlight was blue. Sorry-oo sat alone in the snow, howling. He put his muzzle straight up in the air and howled a long and melancholy song.

'Why don't you go to bed?' asked Moomintroll.

Sorry-oo looked at him with eyes that shone green in the moonlight. One ear was pointing straight up while

the other listened to one side. His whole face was listening.

Very faintly they could hear the howl of hunting
wolves. Sorry-oo nodded bleakly and pulled his woollen
cap on again.

'My great, strong brethren,' he whispered. 'How I
long to be with them.'

'Aren't you afraid of them?' asked Moomintroll.

'Yes, I am,' said Sorry-oo. 'That's the sad part.' He
slunk off along the path to the bathing-house.

Moomintroll crept back into the drawing-room.

A Little Creep had been frightened by the mirror and
sat sobbing in the meerschaum tram.

Otherwise everything was silent.

'What troubles people have,' Moomintroll thought.
'Perhaps the jam isn't such an awful matter, after all.
And I could always put the Sunday jar aside. The straw-
berry one. For the time being.'

*

At dawn the following day the valley was awakened by clear and piercing bugle notes. My sát up at once in her cave, and her feet started to beat time. Too-ticky pricked her ears, and Sorry-oo rushed under one of the benches, with his tail between his legs.

Moomintroll's ancestor annoyedly rattled the damper, and most of the guests woke up.

Moomintroll rushed to the window and crawled out through the snow-tunnel.

The pale winter sun shone over a big Hemulen who came rushing down the nearest slope on his skis. He was holding a shining brass horn to his snout, and seemed to be having a splendid time.

'That one's going to eat lots of jam,' Moomintroll thought. 'And *whatever* are those things he's got on his feet?'

The Hemulen laid his bugle on the woodshed roof and took off his skis.

'Good slopes you have hereabouts,' he said. 'Got any slalom here?'

'I'll ask,' said Moomintroll.

He crawled back to the drawing-room and asked:

'Is there anybody here by name of Slalom?'

'My name's Salome,' whispered the Creep who had been frightened by the mirror.

Moomintroll went back out to the Hemulen and said: 'Almost, but not quite. Here's one Salome.'

But the Hemulen was sniffing about in Moomin-pappa's tobacco plot and didn't listen. 'This is the place for a house,' he said. 'We'll make an igloo here.'

'You might move into my house,' Moomintroll said lingeringly.

'Thanks, never,' replied the Hemulen. 'Too stuffy and unhealthy. I want fresh air, and lots of it. Let's start at once and not lose any time.'

Moomintroll's guests were beginning to crawl outside. They stopped and stood staring.

'Won't he play some more?' asked Salome the Little Creep.

'There's a time for everything, young lady,' said the Hemulen briskly. 'This is the time for a spot of work.'

A little later all the guests were busy building an igloo on Moominpappa's tobacco plot. The Hemulen himself was enjoying a swim in the river, with a couple of chilled Creep as terrified spectators.

Moomintroll went running down to the bathing-house at top-speed.

'Too-ticky!' he shouted. 'There's a Hemulen here . . .

He's going to live in an igloo, and at this moment he's *bathing* in the river.'

'Oh, *that* kind of Hemulen,' Too-ticky said earnestly. 'Then good-bye to peace and all that.' She laid her fishing-rod aside.

On their way back they met Little My who beamed with excitement. 'Seen what he's got?' she cried. 'They're called skis! I'm going to get myself a pair exactly like them at once!'

The igloo was already taking shape. The guests drudged for all they were worth, all the while throwing longing looks towards the jam-cellar. The Hemulen was doing gymnastics down by the river. 'Isn't the cold wonderful?' he said. 'I'm never in such good shape as in winter. Won't you have a dip before breakfast?'

Moomintroll stared at the Hemulen's sweater. It was black and lemon-yellow and zigzaggy. He wondered, slightly troubled, why he couldn't find the Hemulen a jolly person. Although he had been longing and longing for somebody who wouldn't be secretive and distant but cheery and tangible, exactly like the Hemulen.

And now he was feeling more a stranger to the Hemulen than even to the angry and incomprehensible beast under the sink.

He looked helplessly at Too-ticky. She was pouting her underlip and looking at her mitten with raised eyebrows. From this Moomintroll knew that Too-ticky didn't like the Hemulen either. He turned to the Hemulen and said with all the kindness of a bad conscience: 'It must be wonderful to like cold water.'

'I love it,' replied the Hemulen, beaming at him. 'It puts a stop to all unnecessary thoughts and fancies. Believe me: there's nothing more dangerous in life than to become an indoor sitter.'

'Oh?' said Moomintroll.

'Yes. It gives you all kinds of ideas,' said the Hemulen. 'What time's breakfast here?'

'When I've caught some fish,' Too-ticky said sullenly.

'I never eat fish,' said the Hemulen. 'Only vegetables and berries.'

'Cranberry jam?' Moomintroll asked hopefully. The large jar of mashed cranberries had not been popular.

But the Hemulen replied: 'No. Preferably strawberry.'

After breakfast the Hemulen donned his skis and went up the highest of the near-by slopes, the one that started on the hill-top and passed the cave. Down in the valley stood all the guests, looking on. They were a little uncertain of what to think. They tramped about in the snow and wiped their noses now and then, because it was a very cold day.

Now the Hemulen came hurtling downhill. It looked terrifying. Halfway down the slope he swerved in a cloud of glittering snowdust and careered off in another direction. Then he gave a shout and swerved back again. Now he was rushing one way, and now another, and his black-and-yellow sweater made one's eyes water.

Moomintroll closed his eyes and thought: 'How very different people are.'

Little My was already standing at the top of the hill, shouting from joy and admiration. She had broken a barrel and fastened two of the staves under her boots.

'Here I come,' she cried. Without a moment's hesitation Little My set out, straight down the hill. Moomintroll looked up with one eye and saw that she would manage it. Her ferocious little face bore the mark of happy confidence and her legs were stiff as pegs.

Suddenly Moomintroll felt very proud. Little My never shied, she hurtled at breakneck speed close to a pine-bole, wobbled, caught her balance again, and with a roar of laughter threw herself down in the snow beside Moomintroll.

'She's one of my oldest friends,' he explained to the Fillyjonk.

'I believe you,' replied the Fillyjonk sourly. 'What time are elevenses here?'

The Hemulen came plodding over to them. He had taken off his skis, and his snout was glistening from

86

friendliness and warmth. 'Now let's teach Moomin how to ski,' he said.

'I'd prefer not, thanks,' Moomintroll mumbled and shrank back a little. He looked around for Too-ticky. But she had gone, perhaps to catch another kettle of fish.

'The main thing's to keep cool, whatever happens,' the Hemulen was saying encouragingly and already fastening the skis to Moomintroll's paws.

'But I don't want to ...' Moomintroll began miserably.

Little My was looking at him with raised eyebrows.

'Oh, well,' he said bleakly. 'But no high hill.'

'No, no, just the slope down to the bridge,' the Hemulen said. 'Bend your knees. Lean forward. Don't let the skis slip apart. Keep a straight back. Arms close to body. Can you remember what I've told you?'

'No,' said Moomintroll.

He felt a push in the back, closed his eyes and started off. First his skis ran as far away as possible from each other. Then they came together again and mixed themselves up with his ski-sticks. On top of the mixture lay Moomintroll in a strange position.

The guests cheered up.

'Patience is very necessary,' said the Hemulen. 'Oops-a-daisy, and let's do it again.'

'Legs feel a bit shaky,' muttered Moomintroll. This was almost worse than the lonely kind of winter. Even the sun, the so-much-longed-for, was shining straight down into the valley, looking at his humiliation.

Now the bridge came rushing at him up the hill. Moomintroll stuck out one leg to save his balance. The other leg went skiing on. The guests gave a cheer and were beginning to find some fun in life again.

Nothing was up any more, and nothing was down. Nothing existed but snow and misery and disaster everywhere.

Then, finally, Moomintroll found himself hanging in the willow-bushes by the river. His tail was trailing in the icy water, and the water was filled with skis and sticks and new, hostile perspectives.

'Won't do to lose your pluck,' the Hemulen kindly remarked. 'Next time does it!'

But there was no next time, because Moomintroll lost

his pluck. Yes, he really did it, and many times much later he had a dream about how he'd felt that third, triumphant time. He'd have swerved up to the bridge in a sweeping curve, and then stopped and turned round towards the others with a smile. And they'd have shouted in admiration. But now things didn't go that way at all.

Instead Moomintroll said: 'I'm going home. Ski all you care to, but I'm going home.'

And without looking at anybody he crawled into the snow-tunnel and into his warm drawing-room, and farthest into his nest under the rocking chair.

He could hear the Hemulen's whoops from the hill. Moomintroll put his head inside the stove and whispered: 'I don't like him either.'

The ancestor threw down a flake of soot, perhaps to show his sympathy. Moomintroll took a piece of coal and began peacefully to draw on the back of the sofa. He drew a Hemulen standing on his head in a snowdrift. And inside the stove stood a large jar of strawberry jam.

*

During the following week Too-ticky sat doggedly under the ice with her fishing-rod. Beside her under the green ceiling sat a row of guests, also angling. Those were the guests that disliked the Hemulen. Inside the Moomin-house, by and by, gathered all who didn't care to, weren't able to or didn't dare to remonstrate.

Early in the mornings the Hemulen used to put in his head, and a burning torch, at the broken window. He liked torches and camp-fires – and who doesn't? – but he always put them in the wrong place, as it were.

The guests loved their long, somewhat slovenly fore-noons, when the new day was allowed to break later, while everybody discussed the dreams of the night and listened to Moomintroll making coffee in the kitchen.

The Hemulen interrupted all that. He always began by telling them that the drawing-room was stuffy, and de-scribed the fresh cold weather outside.

Then he chatted about what could be done this fine new day. He did his utmost to find some amusements for them all, and he was never hurt when they refused his proposals. He only patted them on the back and said: 'Well, well. You'll see for yourself by and by how right I am.'

The only one who followed him everywhere was Little My. He generously taught her everything he knew about skiing, beaming over her progress.

'Little Miss My,' said the Hemulen. 'You're born on skis. You'll beat me at my own game soon.'

'That's exactly what I figure to do,' replied Little My sincerely. But as soon as she was fully trained, she disappeared to her own hills that nobody knew about, and didn't care much for the Hemulen any more.

As time passed, more and more of the guests became anglers under the ice, and finally the Hemulen's black-and-yellow sweater was the only blob of colour left on the hillside.

The guests didn't like to be involved in new and troublesome things. They liked to sit together talking about old times, before the Lady of the Cold came and they ran out of food. They told each other how they had furnished their homes, and whom they were related to and used to visit, and how terrible the coming of the Great Cold had been, when everything changed.

They shifted closer to the stove, listening to each other and patiently waiting for their own turn to speak.

Moomintroll saw that the Hemulen was left more and more to himself. 'I must get him to leave before he notices it and feels hurt,' Moomintroll thought. 'And before he finishes all the jam.'

But it wasn't easy to find a pretext that would be both believable and tactful.

Sometimes the Hemulen went skiing down to the shore and tried to coax Sorry-oo from the bathing-house. But neither dog-sledge nor even ski-jumping could interest Sorry-oo. He used to sit out all the nights, howling at the moon, and in daytime he was sleepy and wanted to be left alone.

Finally one day the Hemulen thrust his sticks in the snow and said imploringly: 'Don't you see, I like little dogs so terribly much. I've always thought that one day I'd have a dog of my own who would like me too. Why won't you play with me?'

'I really don't know,' Sorry-oo mumbled, blushing. As soon as he had the chance, he slunk back to the bathing-house, and there he continued to dream about the wolves.

It was the wolves he wanted to play with. What boundless happiness, he thought, to hunt with them, to follow them everywhere, to do everything they did and everything they wanted one to do. Then, by and by, he himself would change and become as free and wild as they were.

Every night, when the moonlight glittered in the ice-ferns on the windows, Sorry-oo awoke in the bathing-house and rose to listen. Every night he pulled his woollen cap over his ears and padded softly out.

He took the same path every time, across the sloping shore and into the wood. He continued on his way until the wood became more open and he could see the Lonely Mountains. There Sorry-oo sat down in the snow and waited for the howling of the wolves. Sometimes they were very far away, sometimes nearer. But he heard them neatly every night.

And each time Sorry-oo heard them he put up his muzzle and answered.

Towards morning he crept back again and went to sleep in the bathing-house cupboard.

Too-ticky once looked at him and said: 'You'll never forget them that way.'

'I don't want to forget them,' replied Sorry-oo. 'I want to think of them always.'

*

Strangely enough it was the most timid of them all, Salome the Little Creep, who really liked the Hemulen. She longed to hear him play the horn. But alas! the Hemulen was so big and always in such a hurry that he never noticed her.

No matter how fast she ran he always left her far behind, on his skis, and when she at last overtook the music, it ceased and the Hemulen began doing something else.

A couple of times Salome the Little Creep tried to explain how much she admired him. But she was far too shy and ceremonious, and the Hemulen never had been a good listener.

So nothing of any consequence was said.

One night Salome the Little Creep awoke in the meerschaum tram, where she had settled down on the back gangway. It was no comfortable sleeping-place because of the many buttons and safety-pins the Moomins, in the course of time, had collected in their magnificent drawing-room decoration. And Salome the Little Creep of course was much too considerate to remove them.

Now she could hear Too-ticky and Moomintroll talking under the rocking-chair – and at once she understood that they talked about her beloved Hemulen.

'This is the limit,' said Too-ticky's voice in the dark. 'We simply have to have some peace again. Ever since he started his bugle-tooting my musical shrew has refused to

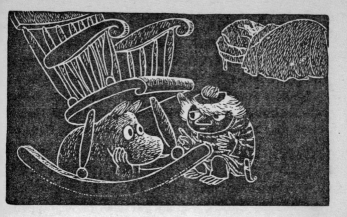

play the flute. Most of my invisible friends have gone away. The guests have a lot of nerves and colds from sitting under the ice all day long. And Sorry-oo hides in the cupboard until nightfall. Somebody has to tell him to leave.'

'I haven't the heart,' said Moomintroll. 'He's so convinced that we like him.'

'Then we'll have to swindle him,' said Too-ticky. 'Tell him the hills in the Lonely Mountains are much higher and better than ours.'

'There are no skiing grounds at all in the Lonely Mountains,' said Moomintroll. 'Only abysses and snaggy cliffs, and not even any snow.'

Salome the Little Creep shivered, and her eyes suddenly filled with tears.

Too-ticky replied: 'Hemulens always manage. And do you suppose it's better to have him understand that we don't like him? Think about it.'

'Can't you do it?' Moomintroll asked wretchedly.

'He lives in your garden, doesn't he?' said Too-ticky. 'Pull yourself together. Everybody'll be the better afterwards. He too.'

Then all was silent. Too-ticky had crawled out through the window.

Salome the Little Creep lay awake and staring out in the darkness. They wanted to send the Hemulen and his horn away. They wanted him to tumble into abysses. There was only one thing to do. He had to be warned against the Lonely Mountains. But cautiously. So that he wouldn't know that people wanted to get rid of him.

Salome the Little Creep lay awake all the night, pondering. Her small head wasn't accustomed to important thoughts like these, and towards morning she was fast asleep. She slept over morning coffee and dinner, and no one even remembered her existence.

*

After breakfast Moomintroll went up to the skiing slope.

'Hello!' cried the Hemulen. 'Fun to see you here! May I teach you a very simple little turn that's not dangerous in the least?'

'Thanks, not today,' said Moomintroll, feeling a big beast. 'I just passed by for a chat.'

'That's great,' said the Hemulen. 'You're not very chatty, none of you, I've noticed. You always seem to be in a hurry and going off somewhere or other.'

Moomintroll cast him a quick look, but the Hemulen looked simply interested and beaming as usual. Moomintroll took a deep breath and said: 'I happen to know that there are some really wonderful hills in the Lonely Mountains.'

'Are there really?' said the Hemulen.

'Oh, yes! Enormous!' Moomintroll continued, nervously. 'The most colossal ups and downs.'

'Ought to give them a try,' said the Hemulen. 'But that's far away. If I'm off to the Lonely Mountains we mightn't meet again this side of spring. And that'd be a pity, wouldn't it?'

'Of course,' Moomintroll replied untruthfully, blushing strongly.

'But really, it's quite an idea,' the Hemulen mused on. '*That* would be outdoor life indeed! The log-fire in the evenings, and new mountain tops to conquer every morning! Long ravine slopes, untouched snow, crisp and rustling under the rushing skis . . .'

The Hemulen lapsed into day-dreams. 'You're really a splendid pal to take such interest in my skiing,' he said thankfully after a while.

Moomintroll stared at him. And then he broke out: 'But they're dangerous hills!'

'Not to me,' said the Hemulen calmly. 'Kind of you

to warn me, but I really love hills. The bigger the better.'

'But they're impossible!' cried Moomintroll, beside himself now. 'Nothing but steep precipices that don't even hold any snow! I told you wrong, I told you wrong! I remember now that somebody told me that it's quite impossible to ski there!'

'Are you sure?' said the Hemulen wonderingly.

'Believe me,' implored Moomintroll. 'Please, won't you stay with us instead? Besides, I've thought about learning to ski . . .'

'Well, in that case,' said the Hemulen. 'If you really want me to stay.'

After his conversation with the Hemulen, Moomintroll was far too upset to go home. Instead he wandered down to the shore and strolled along it. He made a large detour around the bathing-house.

He felt more and more unburdened as he walked along. In the end he was nearly exhilarated. He started to whistle and kicked a lump of ice with great skill along his path. And then it slowly started to snow.

It was the first snow-fall since before New Year, and Moomintroll was greatly surprised.

One flake after the other landed on his warm snout and melted away. He caught several in his paw to admire them for a fleeting moment, he looked towards the sky and saw them sinking down straight at him, more and more, softer and lighter than bird's down.

'Oh, it's like this,' thought Moomintroll. 'I believed it simply formed on the ground somehow.'

The air was milder. There was nothing in sight except falling snow, and Moomintroll was caught by the same

kind of excitement he used to feel at times when he was wading out for a swim. He threw off his bath-gown, and himself headlong in to a snowdrift.

'So that's winter too!' he thought. 'You can even like it!'

*

At dusk Salome the Little Creep awoke with an anxious feeling of being late for something. Then she remembered the Hemulen.

She jumped down from the chest of drawers, first to a chair and then to the floor. The drawing-room was empty. Everybody had gone down to the bathing-house for supper. Salome the Little Creep climbed up to the window and with a lump in her throat crawled through the tunnel.

No moon was up, and no northern lights were showing. There was nothing but densely falling snow that stuck to her face and dress and hindered her steps. She groped her way to the Hemulen's igloo and looked inside. It was dark and forlorn.

At this Salome the Little Creep was seized with a panic, and instead of waiting at the igloo she set out into the whirling snow.

She cried for her beloved Hemulen, but it was like trying to cry through eider-down quilts. Her tracks were next to invisible and very soon hid by the falling snow.

*

Later in the evening the snow-fall stopped.

It was as if a light curtain had been drawn away, and there was a clear view again over the ice. Far out a dark-blue wall of clouds was still hiding the place where the sun had set.

Moomintroll watched the new and threatening weather rolling nearer. The sky darkened suddenly again. Moomintroll who had never seen a blizzard expected a thunderstorm and braced himself against the first claps of thunder that he thought would soon ring out.

But no thunder came, and no lightning either.

Instead a small whirl of snow rose from the white cap of one of the boulders by the shore.

Worried gusts of wind were rushing to and fro over the ice and whispering in the wood by the shore. The dark-blue wall rose higher, and the gusts became stronger.

Suddenly it was as if a great door had blown wide open, the darkness yawned, and everything was filled with wet, flying snow.

This time it didn't come from above, it darted along the ground. It was howling and shoving like a living thing.

Moomintroll lost his balance and turned a somersault. In a trice his ears were full of snow, and he became frightened.

Time and all the world were lost. Everything he could feel and look at had blown away, only a bewitched whirl of damp and dancing darkness was left.

Any sensible person could have told him that this was the very moment when the long spring was born.

But there didn't happen to be any sensible person on the shore, but only a confused Moomin crawling on all fours against the wind, in a totally wrong direction.

He crawled and crawled, and the snow bunged up his eyes and formed a little drift on his snout. Moomintroll became more and more convinced that this was a trick the winter had decided to play him, with the intention of showing him simply that he couldn't stand it.

First it had taken him in by its beautiful curtain of slowly falling flakes, and then it threw all the beautiful snow in his face at the very moment he believed that he had started to like winter.

By and by Moomintroll became angry.

He straightened up and tried to shout at the gale. He hit out against the snow and also whimpered a little, as there was nobody to hear him.

Then he tired.

He turned his back to the blizzard and stopped fighting it.

Not until then did Moomintroll notice that the wind felt warm. It carried him along into the whirling snow, it made him feel light and almost like flying.

'I'm nothing but air and wind, I'm part of the blizzard,' Moomintroll thought and let himself go. 'It's almost like last summer. You first fight the waves, then you turn around and ride the surf, sailing along like a cork among the little rainbows of the foam, and land laughing and just a little frightened in the sand.'

Moomintroll spread out his arms and flew.

'Frighten me if you can,' he thought happily. 'I'm wise to you now. You're no worse than anything else when one gets to know you. Now you won't be able to pull my leg any more.'

And the winter danced him all along the snowy shore, until he stumbled across the snowed-in landing-stage and ploughed his snout through a snowdrift. When he looked up he saw a faint, warm light. It was the window of the bathing-house.

'Oh, I'm saved,' Moomintroll said to himself, a little crestfallen. 'It's a pity that exciting things always stop happening when you're not afraid of them any more and would like to have a little fun.'

When he opened the door, a wisp of steaming, warm air rushed out in the blizzard, and Moomintroll saw fuzzily that the bathing-house was chock-full of people.

'There's one of them!' someone cried.

'Who else?' asked Moomintroll, drying his face.

'Salome the Little Creep's lost in the blizzard,' said Too-ticky gravely.

A glass of hot syrup came gliding through the air. 'Thanks,' said Moomintroll to the invisible shrew. Then he continued: 'But I've never heard about Salome the Little Creep going out of doors.'

'We don't understand it either,' said the oldest of the Whompers. 'And it's no use hunting for her until the blizzard ceases. She might be anywhere, and very probably she's snowed in.'

'Where's the Hemulen?' asked Moomintroll.

'He's gone out to make a search anyhow,' replied Too-ticky. She added with a slight grin: 'You seem to have had a talk about the Lonely Mountains.'

'Well, what of it?' Moomintroll asked vehemently.

Too-ticky's grin spread out. 'You've got a great gift of persuasion,' she said. 'The Hemulen told us that the skiing grounds in the Lonely Mountains are simply wretched. And he was very happy because we all like him so much.'

'I only meant to tell him . . .' Moomintroll began.

'Take it easy,' said Too-ticky. 'It's even possible that we're beginning to like the Hemulen.'

*

The Hemulen perhaps had not very delicate perceptions, and perhaps he didn't always feel what people around him thought about things. But his scent was even keener than Sorry-oo's. (Besides Sorry-oo's scent was spoiled for the time being by emotional thinking.)

The Hemulen had found a couple of old tennis rackets in the attic and had made himself a pair of snow-shoes. Now he was calmly plodding along through the blizzard, keeping his snout close to the ground and trying to catch a whiff of the faint scent of the smallest Creep he had ever seen.

On his way he looked into his igloo and caught the scent there.

'Why, the little squeak's been looking for me here,' the Hemulen thought, good-naturedly. 'I wonder . . .' And suddenly the Hemulen had a fuzzy memory of Salome the Little Creep trying to tell him something some time but being too shy to do it properly.

While he plodded along through the blizzard he saw one picture after the other with his inner vision: The Creep waiting for him beneath the hill . . . The Creep running in his ski-tracks . . . The Creep nosing at the horn ... And the Hemulen thought, flabbergasted: 'I say, I've been unkind to her!' He didn't feel any prick in his conscience, because Hemulens seldom do. But he became a little more interested in finding Salome the Little Creep.

He now laid himself down on his knees so as not to lose her track. The scent went zigzagging and looping along, exactly as little beasts use to scuttle about when they are muddleheaded from fear. The Creep had even been down on the bridge once and gone dangerously near the edge. Then the scent returned, climbed the hill a bit and suddenly disappeared.

The Hemulen stood thinking for a while, which was no mean effort.

Then he started to dig. He dug for quite a time. And finally he came upon something very small and warm.

'Don't be afraid,' said the Hemulen. 'It's only me.'

He tucked the Creep between shirt and flannel vest, rose and started to plod back to the bathing-house.

On his way back, as a matter of fact, he nearly forgot Salome the Little Creep and thought only of a glass of hot syrup and water.

*

The following day was Sunday, and the gale had calmed down. The weather was warm and cloudy, and people sank up to their ears in snow.

The valley looked as strange as a moonscape. The drifts were enormous, rounded heaps or beautifully curved ridges with edges sharp as knives. Every single twig in the wood carried a large snow-cap. The trees looked most of all like big pastry-cakes made by a very fanciful confectioner.

For once all the guests swarmed out in the snow and arranged an enormous snowball fight. The jam was nearly finished, and it had given them all much strength.

The Hemulen sat on the wood-shed roof, blowing his horn with Salome the happy Creep at his side. He played 'The King's Hemulens' and crowned this favourite piece of his with a special flourish. Then he turned to Moomintroll and said: 'You'll have to promise not to be angry with me, but I've made up my mind to go to the Lonely Mountains, come what may. I'll be back again next winter and teach you to ski, instead.'

'But I told you . . .' Moomintroll began anxiously.

'I know, I know,' the Hemulen interrupted. 'You were quite right, too. But after this blizzard the hills must be splendid. And just think how much fresher the air must be there!'

Moomintroll looked at Too-ticky.

She nodded. It meant: 'Let him go. The thing's settled now and everything is for the best.'

Moomintroll went in and opened the shutters of the porcelain stove. First he softly called to his ancestor, a low signal, somewhat like: Tee-yooo, tee-yooo. The ancestor didn't reply.

'I've neglected him,' Moomintroll thought. 'But things that happen now really *are* more interesting than those that happened a thousand years ago.'

He lifted out the big jar of strawberry jam. Then he

took a piece of charcoal and wrote on the paper lid: 'To my old friend, the Hemulen.'

*

That evening Sorry-oo had to struggle for a whole hour in the snow until he finally reached his wailing pit. Each time he had sat there with his longing, the wailing-pit had grown slightly larger, but now it was set deep in a snowdrift.

The Lonely Mountains were wholly snow-clad now and shone before him in splendid whiteness. The night

was moonless, but the stars were twinkling unusually bright. From far away came the rumbling of an avalanche. Sorry-oo sat down to wait for the wolves.

Tonight he had to wait long.

He imagined them running over snowy fields, grey and big and strong – and then they would suddenly stop when they heard his calling howl from the edge of the wood.

Perhaps they'd think: 'Listen, there's a pal. A cousin we could have for a companion . . .'

This thought made Sorry-oo feel excited, and his imagination carried him further. He embroidered his daydream while he waited. He let the whole pack appear over the nearest hill. They came running towards him . . . They wagged their tails . . . Then Sorry-oo remembered that genuine wolves never wag their tails.

But that was no matter. They came running, they knew him from before . . . They had already decided to take him along with them . . .

Now Sorry-oo was quite overwhelmed with his vivid daydream. He turned his muzzle to the stars and gave a howl.

And the wolves answered him.

They were so near that Sorry-oo felt frightened. He tried clumsily to burrow down in the snow. Eyes were lighting up all around him.

The wolves were silent again. They had formed a ring around him, and it was slowly closing in.

Sorry-oo wagged his tail and whined, but nobody answered him. He took off his woollen cap and threw it in the air to show that he would like to play. That he was quite harmless.

But the wolves didn't even look at the cap. And suddenly Sorry-oo knew that he had made a mistake. They weren't his brethren at all, and one couldn't have any fun with them.

One could only be eaten up, and possibly have the time to regret that one had behaved like an ass. He stopped his tail that was still wagging from pure habit, and thought: 'What a pity. I could have slept all these nights instead of sitting here and longing myself silly...'

The wolves were coming nearer.

At that very moment a clear bugle call resounded through the wood. It was a blaring brass blast that shook lots of snow from the trees and made the yellow eyes blink. Within a second the danger was past and Sorry-oo was alone again beside his woollen cap. On his large snow-shoes the Hemulen came shuffling up the hill.

'Sitting here, are you, little doggie?' said the Hemulen. 'Have you waited long for me?'

'No,' said Sorry-oo truthfully.

'There'll be a fine crust on the snow tonight,' said the Hemulen happily. 'And when we're up on the Lonely Mountains we'll share the nice warm milk I have in my thermos.'

The Hemulen shuffled on, without looking over his shoulder.

Sorry-oo padded after him. It seemed much the best thing he could do.

CHAPTER 6

The first of spring

THE first spring blizzard had brought change and unrest to the valley. The guests became more homesick than ever. One after the other they started back, usually in the night when the snow-crust made walking easy. A few of them had made themselves a pair of skis, and everyone carried at least one little jam-jar with him. The last ones to go shared the cranberry-jar.

As the last of the guests walked off over the bridge, the jam-cellar was completely empty.

'Now it's only we again,' said Too-ticky. 'You and me and Little My. All the mysterious ones have hidden away until next winter.'

'I never saw him with the silver horns a second time,' said Moomintroll. 'Nor those spindle-shanked little ones that came skidding over the ice. Nor the black one who flew over the bonfire and had such large eyes.'

'They were all winter people,' said Too-ticky. 'Can't you feel that spring's coming?'

Moomintroll shook his head. 'It's too early still. I don't recognize it,' he said.

But Too-ticky turned her red cap inside out, and the inside turned out to be a pale blue. 'I always do this when I feel spring in my nose,' she said. Then she seated herself on the lid of the well and sang:

> I am Too-ticky
> And my cap's turned inside out!
> I am Too-ticky
> Catching warm winds in my nose!
> Great blizzards are drawing near!
> Great avalanches roar!
> The great earth revolves
> And everything is changed these days
> Including people's winter woollens.

One evening when Moomintroll was on his way home from the bathing-house he stopped on the path and pricked his ears.

It was a cloudy, warm night, full of movement. The trees had long since shaken off their snow, and he could hear them tossing their branches in the dark.

Far away from the south came a strong gust of wind. He could hear it soughing along through the wood and passing him on its way across the valley.

A little shower of water drops fell from the trees into the darkening snow, and Moomintroll lifted his snout to sniff.

That could have been a faint whiff of bare earth, indeed. He continued on his way and knew that Too-ticky had been right. Spring was really on its way.

For the first time in many weeks Moomintroll went and looked carefully at his sleeping Pappa and Mamma. He also held the lamp over the Snork Maiden and regarded her musingly. Her fringe fluff had a nice gleam in the lamplight. She was very sweet. As soon as she awoke she would rush to the cupboard and look for her green spring hat.

Moomintroll set the lamp on the mantelpiece and looked around him at the drawing-room. It was a horrid sight indeed. Most of the things had been given away, borrowed or simply taken by some thoughtless guest.

The remaining things were in an indescribable jumble. Unwashed dishes were piled high on the kitchen sink. The central-heating fire in the cellar would soon go out, as there was no more peat. The jam-cellar was empty. And a window-pane was broken.

Moomintroll pondered. He could hear the wet snow starting to slide down along the roof above him. It landed with a big thump, and suddenly he could see a piece of the clouded night sky through the upper part of the south window.

Moomintroll went to the main door and felt it. Didn't it give, ever so little? He dug his hind paws in the carpet and applied all his muscle.

Slowly, very slowly the door opened, pushing a large mass of snow outwards before it.

Moomintroll didn't give up until the door stood wide open against the night.

Now the strong wind blew straight into the drawing-room. It shook the dust off the gauze around the chandelier, and it fanned the ashes in the porcelain stove. It flapped the transfers that were pasted on the walls. One of them came off and was carried away.

The room was filled with a smell of night and firs, and Moomintroll thought: 'Good. A family has to be ventilated at times.' He went out on the steps and stared out into the damp darkness.

'Now I've got everything,' Moomintroll said to himself. 'I've got the whole year. Winter too. I'm the first Moomin to have lived through an entire year.'

*

Really, this winter's tale ought to stop exactly at this point. All this about the first spring night, and the wind rushing about in the drawing-room makes a magnificent ending. And then everybody could think what they pleased about what happened afterwards. But that wouldn't be right.

Because one still couldn't be absolutely sure of what Moominmamma had to say when she awoke. Nor would one know whether the ancestor was allowed to settle down for good in the porcelain stove. Nor whether Snufkin was back again before the story ended. Nor how the Mymble had managed without her cardboard box. Nor where Too-ticky would move when the bathing-house became a bathing-house again. Nor a lot of other things.

I suppose it's better to go on.

Especially as the break-up of the ice is an important event and much too dramatic to be left out.

*

Now followed the mysterious month of bright sunny days, of melting icicles, and winds, and rushing skies – and of sharply freezing nights with a snow-crust and a dazzling moon. Moomintroll explored every nook of his valley, dizzy from expectation and pride.

Now came spring, but not at all as he had imagined its coming. He had thought that it would deliver him from a strange and hostile world, but now it was simply a continuation of his new experiences, of something he had already conquered and made his own.

He hoped for a long spring, so that he could have his happy, expectant feeling as long as possible. Every morning he almost dreaded for the second-best that could happen: that someone of the family would awaken. He moved cautiously and tried not to bump into things in the drawing-room. And early in the morning he went scuttling out in the valley, to sniff the new smells and to look at the changes since the day before.

By the south wall of the woodshed an ever-widening spot of earth was becoming bare. The birches were showing a faint shade of red, but it could be seen only at a distance. The sun had burned right through the snow-drifts, and made them honeycombed and brittle. And the ice was darkening, as if the sea was beginning to show through.

Little My still went skating about far out. She had changed her tin lids for kitchen knives and managed to fasten them edgewise under her boots.

Now and then Moomintroll came across a figure eight she had made in the ice, but very seldom did he see her. She had always had the gift of having fun on her own, and whatever she might have been thinking about spring she felt no need to talk about it.

Too-ticky was having a spring cleaning in the bathing-house.

She rubbed all the green and red panes bright for the first summer fly, she hung out the bath-gowns in the sun and tried to repair the rubber Hemulen.

'Now the bathing-house'll be a bathing-house again,' she said. 'When the summer's hot and green, and you lie on your tummy on the warm boards of the landing-stage and listen to the waves chuckling and clucking . . .'

'Why didn't you talk like that in winter,' said Moomintroll. 'It'd have been such a comfort. Remember, I said once: "There were a lot of apples here." And you just replied: "But now here's a lot of snow." Didn't you understand that I was melancholy?'

Too-ticky shrugged her shoulders. 'One has to dis-

cover everything for oneself,' she replied. 'And get over it all alone.'

The sun was more and more burning every day.

It bored the ice full of small holes and channels, and one could see that the sea was becoming restless below.

Beyond the horizon great gales were wandering to and fro.

Moomintroll lay awake late at nights, listening to the creakings and crackings in the walls of the sleeping house.

The ancestor was very quiet. He had closed the shutters behind him and perhaps retired again a thousand years back. The damper cord had disappeared into the

cranny between the stove and the wall, tassels, embroidery and all.

'He liked it,' Moomintroll thought. He had moved
from the basket of wool and was sleeping in his own bed

again. In the mornings the sun shone farther and farther
into the drawing-room, looking embarrassedly at cob-
webs and dust pellets. The bigger dust wads, those that
had grown round and full of personality, Moomintroll
used to carry out on the veranda, but the small ones he
allowed to roll about as they liked.

The earth under the south window was becoming
quite warm in the afternoon. It looked slightly bulging

from brown, bursting bulbs and from the many small root threads that were eagerly sucking at the melting snow.

And then one windy day, a little before dusk, a strong and majestic report was heard far out to sea.

'Well,' said Too-ticky and put her teacup down. 'The spring cannonade's starting.'

The ice heaved, and more reports thundered.

Moomintroll ran out from the bathing-house to listen in the warm wind.

'Look, the sea's coming in,' said Too-ticky behind him.

Far out a white border of waves was hissing, angry and hungry waves biting off piece after piece of the winter ice.

A black crack came shooting in along the ice, it wove to and fro, and then it tired and disappeared. The sea heaved again and new cracks formed. They broadened.

'I know someone who'd better hurry up and come home,' said Too-ticky.

Little My of course had noticed that something was about to happen. But she simply couldn't leave off. She had to take a look, out where the sea had broken free. So

she had skated up to the outermost edge and cut a proud figure of eight in the face of the sea.

Then she turned about and went back at top speed over the cracking ice. At first the cracks were quite thin. 'Danger', they were writing all over the ice, as far as she could see.

The ice sagged, heaved and sank again, and every now and then thundered the cannon salute of festivity and destruction that sent delightful cold thrills up her back.

'I hope the silly asses won't be hopping out here to save me,' she thought. 'That'd spoil everything.' She went full speed ahead, nearly doubled up on her kitchen knives. The shore didn't seem to come any nearer.

Now some of the cracks were widening and becoming streams. An angry little wave lashed out.

And then suddenly the sea was filled with rocking ice islands that knocked against each other in confusion. On one of them stood Little My, looking at the stretches of water all around her, and she thought without any special alarm: 'Well, this is a pretty go.'

Moomintroll was already on his way out to her rescue. Too-ticky stood looking on for a while, and then she went inside the bathing-house and put a kettle of water on the stove. 'Quite, quite,' she thought with a little sigh. 'It's always like this in their adventures. To save and be saved. I wish somebody would write a story sometime about the people who warm up the heroes afterwards.'

As Moomintroll ran he watched a small crack running alongside him. It was keeping abreast of him.

The ice heaved in the swell, and suddenly it broke in pieces and started rocking violently under his feet.

Little My was standing quite still on her ice-floe, watching the jumping Moomintroll. He looked exactly like a bouncing rubber ball, and his eyes were round from excitement and strain. When he landed at her side Little My held up her arms and said: 'Put me on your head, will you, so I can get off if I must?'

Then she grabbed a sure hold of his ears and cried: ' "A" company, towards the shore, *turn*!'

Moomintroll threw a quick glance at the bathing-house. The chimney was smoking, but not a soul was to be seen on the landing-stage, wringing its hands from worry. He hesitated, and his legs suddenly felt heavy from disappointment.

'Off we go!' shouted Little My.

And Moomintroll set out. He jumped and he jumped, with set teeth and on shaky legs. Every time he landed on a new floe a cold shower washed his tummy.

The whole stretch of ice was broken now, and the waves were waltzing all the way to the shore.

'Keep in step!' shouted Little My. 'Here's one again ... you'll feel it under you ... *jump*!'

And Moomintroll jumped, at the exact moment when the wave gently pushed an ice-floe under his paws. 'One, two, three; *one*, two three,' Little My was counting in waltz time. '*One*, two, three, wait – *one*, two, three – *jump*!'

Moomintroll's legs were shaky and his stomach cold as ice. A red sunset was breaking through the cloudy sky, and the gleam of the waves hurt his eyes. He felt hot all down his back, but his stomach was cold and the whole cruel world was swirling dizzily before his eyes.

Too-ticky had kept an earnest look-out in the window of the bathing-house, and she saw now that things were going badly.

'Stupid of me,' she thought. 'Of course he can't know that I've been looking on all the time . . .'

She rushed out on the landing-stage and cried: 'Oh, well done sir!'

But it was already too late.

The last, lonely jump had been too much for Moomin-

troll, and he suddenly found himself floating in the sea with water up to his ears, while a spirited little ice-floe kept knocking him in the back of his neck.

Little My had let go of his ears and taken a last long jump ashore. It is strange how deftly people like the Mys get on in life.

'Catch hold,' said Too-ticky, reaching out a steady paw. She lay on her stomach on Moominmamma's wash-board and looked straight in Moomintroll's troubled eyes.

'There, there,' she said. Slowly Moomintroll was dragged up over the ice-edge, and slowly he crawled inwards over the boulders by the water. He said: 'You didn't even care to look on.'

'I watched you through the window all the time,' Too-ticky replied worriedly. 'Now you'd better come inside and warm yourself.'

'No, I'm going home,' said Moomintroll. He rose to his feet and staggered off.

'Warm syrup!' Too-ticky shouted after him. 'Don't forget to drink something warm!'

The path was wet from melting snow, and Moomintroll could feel roots and pine needles under his paws. But he was shaking from cold, and his legs felt slithery, like rubber.

He hardly turned his head as a small squirrel jumped across his path.

'Happy spring,' said the squirrel, absentmindedly.

'Well, thanks,' replied Moomintroll and continued on his way. But all at once he stopped short and stared at the squirrel. It had a big and bushy tail that shone red in the sunset.

'Do people call you the squirrel with the marvellous tail?' Moomintroll asked slowly.

'Of course,' said the squirrel.

'Is it you?' cried Moomintroll. 'Is it really you? Who met the Lady of the Cold?'

'I don't remember,' said the squirrel. 'You know, I'm not very bright at remembering things.'

'But try to,' begged Moomintroll. 'Don't you even remember the nice mattress that was stuffed with wool?'

The squirrel scratched his left ear. 'I remember a lot of mattresses,' he replied. 'With wool, and other stuffings. Wool ones are nicest.'

And the squirrel skipped off between the trees.

'I'll have to look into this later,' thought Moomintroll. 'For the moment I'm too cold. I have to go home . . .'

And he sneezed, because he had got a bad cold for the first time in his life.

The central-heating fire had gone out, and the drawing-room was very chilly.

With shaking paws Moomintroll heaped several carpets over his stomach, but they didn't make him feel any warmer. He had a pain in his legs and felt a pricking in his throat. All of a sudden life was sad, and his snout felt strange and enormous. He tried to curl his ice-cold tail, and he sneezed again.

At this his Mamma awoke.

She hadn't heard the thunder of the breaking ice and never once the howls of the blizzards. Her house had been filled with restless guests, but neither they nor the alarm clock had been able to wake her.

Now she opened her eyes and looked up at the ceiling, wide awake.

Then she sat up in bed and said: 'You've caught a cold, Moomintroll.'

'Mamma,' Moomintroll said between chattering teeth, 'if I were only sure it was the same squirrel and not another one.'

Moominmamma hurried out to the kitchen to warm some syrup.

'Nobody's washed the dishes,' Moomintroll cried wretchedly.

'Oh, of course not,' said Moominmamma. 'Everything's going to be all right.'

She found a few sticks of wood behind the slop-pail. She took a bottle of currant syrup from her secret cupboard, as well as a powder and a flannel scarf.

When the water boiled she mixed a strong influenza

medicine of sugar and ginger, and an old lemon that used to lie behind the tea-cosy on the topmost shelf but one.

There was no tea-cosy, nor any teapot. But Moominmamma never noticed that. For safety's sake she mumbled a short charm over the influenza medicine. That was something her grandmother had taught her. Then she went back to the drawing-room and said: 'Please drink it as hot as you can.'

Moomintroll drank and felt a mild warmth flowing through his tummy. 'Mamma,' he said, 'there's such a lot to explain to you ...'

'First take a nap,' Moominmamma said and wound the flannel around his throat.

'Just one thing,' Moomintroll mumbled sleepily. 'Promise not to have a fire in the porcelain stove, because our ancestor's living there now.'

'Of course not,' said Moominmamma.

All at once Moomintroll felt warm and calm and free of responsibility. He sighed a little and burrowed his snout in the pillow. Then he fell asleep, away from it all.

*

Moominmamma sat on the verandah burning a strip of film with a magnifying glass. The film smoked and glowed, and a nice pungent smell was tickling her snout.

The sun was so warm that the wet verandah steps were steaming, but the shadow beside them was ice-cold.

'One really ought to get up a little earlier in the spring,' remarked Moominmamma.

'You're very right,' said Too-ticky. 'Is he still asleep?' Moominmamma nodded.

'You ought to have seen him jump the ice-floes!' Little My said proudly. 'And he had sat half the winter just whining and pasting transfers on the walls.'

'I know, I've seen them,' said Moominmamma. 'He must have felt very lonely.'

'Then he went and found some kind of an old ancestor of yours,' Little My continued.

'Let him tell the story himself when he awakes,' said Moominmamma. 'I can see that lots of things have happened while I slept.'

The film was finished, and she managed to burn a round, black hole in the verandah flooring as well.

'I must get up before the others next spring,' Moominmamma said. 'How nice to be on your own for a bit
and do what you like.'

*

When Moomintroll finally awoke, his throat wasn't sore
any longer.

He noticed that Moominmamma had taken the gauze
off the chandelier and put up the window curtains. The
furniture was moved back to its usual places, and the
broken pane had been repaired with a piece of cardboard. Not a dust-wad was in sight.

Only the ancestor's rubbish in front of the porcelain
stove was untouched. Moominmamma had put up a tidy
placard on it:

DO NOT DISTURB

From the kitchen came the cosy sounds of dishes
being washed.

'Shall I tell her about the Dweller Under the Sink?'
Moomintroll thought. 'Perhaps I'd better not . . .' He lay
for a while wondering whether he'd be ill a little longer
and have Moominmamma nurse him a little more. But
then he decided that it would be nicer still to take care of
Moominmamma himself. He went out to the kitchen and
said:

'Let me show you the snow!'

Moominmamma at once stopped washing dishes and
they walked out into the sunlight together.

'There's not so much left of it now,' Moomintroll ex-

131

plained. 'But you should have seen it in winter! The snowdrifts reached up to the roof! You could hardly take a step without sinking up to your snout! Do you know, when the snow comes it falls down from the sky like tiny and very cold stars. And up there in the black sky you can see fluttering blue and green curtains.'

'That sounds nice,' replied Moominmamma.

'Yes, and even if you can't walk on the snow you can slide along on it,' continued Moomintroll. 'It's called skiing. It makes you rush ahead fast, like lightning, in a cloud of whirling snow, and you've got to look sharp, or else.'

'You don't say,' said Moominmamma. 'Is that where you use trays?'

'No, they're better on the ice,' her son mumbled, a little taken aback.

'Really, really,' said Moominmamma, squinting at the sun. 'Life is very charming, I must say. Here one has believed all one's life that there's just one use for a silver tray, and then it appears to be still better for quite another purpose. And every year people are telling me that I give myself far too much trouble making such lots of jam – and then all of a sudden it's all gone!'

Moomintroll blushed. 'Has Little My told you about. . . ?' he asked.

'Yes,' said Moominmamma. 'Thank goodness that you took care of the people so I wasn't put to shame. And do you know, I really believe that the house'll be a lot airier without such a lot of carpets and odds and ends. Besides, it makes cleaning very much simpler.'

Moominmamma scooped up a handful of snow and made a snowball. She threw it clumsily as mothers do, and it plopped to the ground not very far away.

'I'm no good at that,' said Moominmamma with a laugh. 'Even Sorry-oo would have made a better throw.'

'Mother, I love you terribly,' said Moomintroll.

They went strolling slowly down to the bridge, but no mail had come yet. The evening sun threw long shadows through the valley, and all was calm with a wonderful peace.

Moominmamma seated herself on the bridge parapet and said:

'And now I'd like to hear something about our ancestor.'

*

The following morning the whole family awoke at the same time. They were awakened in exactly the right way: by a merrily tinkling barrel-organ.

Too-ticky was turning the crank, standing under the dripping roof-edge in her sky-blue cap that was turned inside out. The sky itself was no lighter blue. The silver mountings on her barrel-organ glinted in the sun.

At her side sat Little My, half-proud and half-embarrassed, because she had tried with her own paws to repair the tea-cosy, and she had scoured the silver tray with sand. Neither article had fared quite well from it, but, very probably, intentions are more important than results.

At some distance the sleepy Mymble was seen to approach, dragging after her the drawing-room carpet in which she had slept through the winter.

This day the spring had decided not to be poetical but simply cheerful. It had spread flocks of small scatter-brained clouds in the sky, it swept down the last specks of snow from every roof, it made new little brooks run everywhere and was playing at April the best it could.

'I'm awake!' cried the Snork Maiden expectantly. Moomintroll kindly brushed his snout against hers and said: 'Happy spring!' At the same time he wondered whether he would ever be able to tell her about his winter so that she'd understand it.

He saw her run straight to the cupboard to take out her green spring bonnet.

He saw his Daddy eagerly collect wind-gauge and spade and step out on the verandah.

All the time Too-ticky's barrel-organ was playing and the sunlight streaming down into the valley, as if the elements were sorry for having shown their own subjects such unfriendliness in the past.

'Snufkin'll be here today,' thought Moomintroll. 'It's exactly the right kind of day for him to arrive.'

He stood on the verandah and looked at the family. They were hopping around in the garden plot, dizzy with merriment, as at every spring.

He caught Too-ticky's eye. She cranked the waltz to an end, laughed and said: 'Now the bathing-house is vacant again!'

'I'm of the opinion that the only one who can live in the bathing-house after this is Too-ticky herself,' said Moominmamma. 'To have a bathing-house is a bit coddling, really. One can just as well step into one's trunks on the shore.'

'Thanks,' said Too-ticky. 'I'll think about it.'

And she went on her way down the valley to awaken all the other sleeping Creeps and beasts with her barrel-organ.

But the Snork Maiden had come across the first brave nose-tip of a crocus. It was pushing through the warm spot under the south window, but wasn't even green yet.

'Let's put a glass over it,' said the Snork Maiden. 'It'll be better off in the night if there's a frost.'

'No, don't do that,' said Moomintroll. 'Let it fight it out. I believe it's going to do still better if things aren't so easy.'

Suddenly he felt so happy that he had to be alone. He strolled off towards the woodshed.

And when nobody could see him any longer he broke into a run. He ran through the melting snow, with the sun warming his back. He ran simply because he was happy, with nothing at all to think about.

He ran on down to the shore and out on the landing-stage and straight through the empty, aired bathing-house.

Then he seated himself on the bathing-house steps, with the spring sea at his feet.

He could only just hear the barrel-organ playing in the farthest corner of the valley, if he listened very closely.

Moomintroll looked down in the water and tried to remember the time when the ice had stretched away and melted into the darkness of the horizon.

**THE END AND
THE BEGINNING**

FINN FAMILY MOOMINTROLL

The first book about Moomins. They live in the forests of Finland, sleep through the winter and have many adventures, which start when Moomintroll finds the Hobgoblin Hat.

COMET IN MOOMINLAND

Moomintroll and Sniff set out for the Observatory on the Lonely Mountain to ask the Professor if a comet is really on its way to destroy the Earth.

THE EXPLOITS OF MOOMINPAPPA

The story of Moominpappa's life, beginning with his arrival on the doorstep of the foundlings home, wrapped in newspaper, continuing with his running away, his adventures round the world, and the rescue of the beautiful future Moominmamma.

MOOMINSUMMER MADNESS

The Moomin family, flooded out of their old home, take like ducks to water to play-acting in a floating theatre instead.

MOOMINPAPPA AT SEA

Moominpappa is restless at home in Moominvalley, and takes his family to live on a lonely mysterious island where life will be more of a challenge.

TALES FROM MOOMINVALLEY

Nine more fascinating, deliciously humorous and haunting stories from the realms of Moominland.

MOOMINVALLEY IN NOVEMBER

Winter is coming, and the Fillyjonk, the Hemulen, Toft, Mymble, etc. are all waiting in Moominvalley to see the Moomins return home, for winter doesn't seem right without them.